ECHOES OF IMAGINATION

Where Love Defies Boundaries, and Destiny Whispers Through Time

BRIAN MIRANDA

Dedication

To my dearest daughter, Xenia,

You are the greatest story my heart will ever tell. May your imagination always lead you to places where dreams take flight, where wonder knows no bounds, and where the echoes of your creativity inspire the world around you. Never stop believing in the beauty of possibility—for it lives within you.

With all my love,
Dad

CONTENTS

[The First]
Whispers in the Monsoon

[The Second]
The Reunion of Hearts

FOREWORD

When Brian first asked me to write this foreword, I felt honored—but more than that, I felt intrigued. What awaited me within these pages was not just a collection of stories but a journey through the extraordinary landscapes of imagination, memory, and belief.

Reading Echoes of Imagination is like stepping into a world where the lines between reality and perception blur, where the familiar transforms into something profound. Brian has a rare ability—to craft stories that not only immerse but also invite reflection. As I read, I wasn't merely an observer; I was a silent presence in every scene, feeling the pulse of each moment as if it were unfolding around me.

There's something deeply evocative about these stories. They are not just narrations; they are experiences—woven with emotions, unanswered questions, and the kind of details that linger in the mind long after you turn the last page. The beauty of this book is that each reader will find their own meaning within its depths. The words are not rigid; they are fluid, allowing space for interpretation, introspection, and even nostalgia.

The attention to detail is remarkable, yet it never overwhelms. Instead, it guides, leading the reader to fill in the gaps with their own thoughts and emotions. The "missing pieces" aren't missing at all—they exist in the spaces between the lines, waiting to be uncovered by those willing to look beyond what is written.

For those who have ever found themselves lost in the transitions of time, whether between cities or within their own hearts, this book will resonate deeply. For those who seek stories that challenge perspectives, Echoes of Imagination will be a revelation.

This isn't just a book. It's an invitation—to dream, to wonder, and to embrace the echoes of your own imagination.

Happy reading, and may this be just the beginning of many more stories to come.

– Ameet Dighe

PREFACE

It is with great joy and a deep sense of fulfilment that I present to you *Echoes of Imagination*, a collection of four short stories that has been a labour of love over the past year. The journey of crafting these tales has been one of immense growth, reflection, and discovery, as each story emerged from a blend of personal experience, imagination, and the inspiration drawn from the world and people around me.

First and foremost, I owe my deepest gratitude to Lord God, my Heavenly Father. All praise, glory, and honour to the Almighty, for without His grace, guidance, and blessings, this endeavour would not have been possible. He has been my source of strength, wisdom, and creativity throughout this journey, and to Him, I glorify my efforts.

Through these stories, I have sought to capture echoes of emotions, dreams, and reflections that resonate universally. Each tale offers a glimpse into diverse lives and perspectives, exploring the human experience through themes of love, loss, hope, and imagination. Though distinct in tone and narrative, they are united by their shared purpose: to leave a lasting impression and invite readers to reflect on the beauty and complexity of life.

The title, *Echoes of Imagination,* was chosen to reflect this duality—the act of creating worlds through imagination and the lasting reverberation of stories in the hearts of those who read them. *"Echoes"* represents the lingering impact of storytelling, while *"Imagination"* celebrates the boundless creativity that allows us to dream, explore, and connect.

This book would not have been possible without the unwavering support, encouragement, and generosity of some truly wonderful individuals, to whom I am forever grateful.

Amidst them, there is one person whose love and sacrifice have been the foundation of all that I am today—my mother. She has been my constant anchor, guiding me with her wisdom and lifting me with her unwavering faith. Her prayers, patience, and quiet strength have shaped my journey in ways beyond measure. To my dearest mom, thank you for being my greatest source of love, support, and inspiration.

ACKNOWLEDGEMENTS

To **Ameet Dighe**, thank you for being the driving force behind the start of this project. Your constant encouragement and belief in my ability to write gave me the courage to take that first step. Your faith in my potential has been a guiding light, and for that, I am deeply thankful.

To **Joseph Mascarenhas**, your artistic brilliance brought my vision for the cover to life. The beautiful cover that now graces this book is a testament to your creativity and skill. Your contribution to this project is something I will always cherish.

To **Mary Rebeiro**, your thoughtful guidance and suggestions for the imagery helped shape the worlds I sought to create. Your keen eye for detail, insightful feedback, and unwavering support played a crucial role in bringing depth and vibrancy to this collection. You didn't just offer suggestions—you helped refine and elevate the very essence of these stories, making them more vivid and emotionally resonant. Your generosity of spirit and willingness to share your wisdom have left an indelible mark on this book, and for that, I am profoundly grateful.

To **G & Carol**, your incredible talent behind the lens turned a simple photo-shoot into something truly special. Thank you for capturing me in a way that reflects the essence of this journey. Your work has given me a profile that represents not just an author, but the emotions and passion behind *Echoes of Imagination*.

To the **whole team at Notion Press**, my heartfelt gratitude for your meticulous attention to detail, your constant suggestions, and your drive to ensure that this book became the best version of itself. A special thank you to **Isha & Harshita**—your dedication, patience, and keen editorial insight have made this book stronger than I could have imagined. I truly appreciate your unwavering support throughout this process.

Holding the final published book in my hands fills me with a deep sense of gratitude. Every bit of effort, refinement, and care that went into shaping this collection has made it all the more special, and I couldn't be more grateful to have had such a committed team by my side.

To **Pastor Satish and Pastor Alex**, thank you for your prayers, wisdom, and unwavering support. Your guidance has been a source of strength in my faith and personal journey, and your encouragement has meant more to me than words can express. The impact of your teachings and mentor-ship extends far beyond the pulpit, and I am truly grateful for your presence in my life.

To **a few extraordinary women**, though I have chosen not to name you here, your strength, grace, and resilience have inspired the female characters in these stories. You have profoundly shaped my understanding of the human spirit, and I hope you see glimpses of yourselves in the pages of this book. I offer you my deepest respect and gratitude for inspiring me in ways that words alone cannot express.

Special Acknowledgment

To **Tony Valechha**, thank you for your unwavering support and inspiration in my professional endeavors. Your constant encouragement, insightful conversations, and creation of opportunities to write valuable papers have been instrumental in my growth. Your faith in my abilities gave me the confidence to embark on this literary journey, and for that, I am eternally grateful.

Writing *Echoes of Imagination* has been a deeply personal and trans-formative experience. It has allowed me to pour out my heart, explore the uncharted corners of my imagination, and reflect on the people and moments that have left an indelible mark on my life.

As I hold the final published book in my hands, I am filled with an overwhelming sense of fulfillment. Every moment spent crafting these stories, every challenge faced along the way, and every bit of effort poured into this collection has culminated in something I am incredibly proud to share with you.

My greatest hope is that these stories find a place in your heart. May they offer moments of connection, inspiration, and perhaps even a spark of wonder. Thank you for joining me on this journey and for giving these stories a chance to resonate in your world.

With heartfelt gratitude,

Brian Miranda

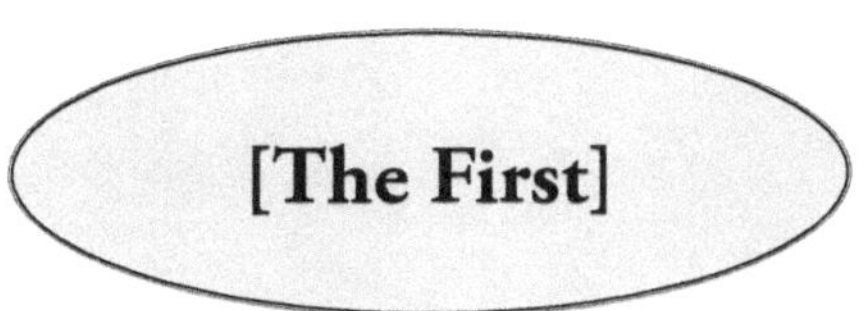

Whispers in the Monsoon

CHAPTER 1

THE DANCER AND THE DREAMER

Bombay 1992

The city swayed under the spell of the monsoon's relentless downpour, transforming its streets into a kaleidoscope of shimmering puddles and vibrant reflections. The rain, cascading in silvery sheets, seemed to breathe life into the bustling metropolis, lending an air of mystique and magic to its winding alleys and crowded boulevards. This year, the monsoon had arrived with a fierce intensity, as if the skies themselves were determined to wash away the grime of the city, leaving behind only purity and promise.

Against this backdrop of rain and rhythm, Bombay's anticipation for Ganesh Chaturthi pulsed like a heartbeat. The city's spirit soared as every lane and byway was adorned with festoons and the rhythmic beat of traditional drums. Temples were bedecked in garlands, while massive pandals, temporary structures of devotion and art, rose from the ground like colourful giants. The aroma of freshly made sweets and the scent of marigold and jasmine mingled with the earthy fragrance of wet soil, creating a heady blend that was uniquely Bombay.

Amidst this fervour, the spotlight was firmly on Meera Kapoor, the city's beloved classical dancer. She was a vision of elegance and poise, her every movement embodying a perfect harmony between tradition and emotion. Tonight, she would perform a dance dedicated to Lord Ganesha, a dance that symbolised the eternal triumph of good over evil. The anticipation in the air was palpable as people crowded the main temple grounds, eager to catch a glimpse of Meera in action. The temple courtyard, transformed into an impromptu auditorium, shimmered in the golden glow of a thousand lanterns. A hush fell over the audience as Meera, dressed in a vibrant crimson saree embroidered with gold, stepped onto the stage. The tiny bells around her ankles jingled softly, a prelude to the powerful rhythm she would soon command.

As the music swelled, Meera's body became an instrument of storytelling. Her movements were precise yet fluid, each gesture carrying layers of meaning. Her eyes sparkled with an intensity that drew the audience in, making them feel every joy, sorrow, and triumph she expressed. To the untrained eye, her dance was a blur of beauty, a mesmerising spectacle. But to those who understood, it was a profound narrative – a dialogue between devotion and desire, duty and defiance. Among those watching was Aarav Deshmukh. A relative newcomer to the city, Aarav was still adjusting to Bombay's chaotic blend of tradition and modernity. A young software engineer, he had left his small town behind in search of new opportunities, and while he had come to appreciate the city's dynamic energy, tonight was the first time he felt truly entranced.

He had been dragged to the performance by a colleague, but now, he was glad for it. There was something about Meera's dance—an ethereal beauty that made the world around him blur into insignificance. His gaze remained fixed on Meera, unable to look away. She was more than just a dancer. She was a force of nature, drawing everyone into her orbit. Each spin, each subtle shift of her fingers, seemed to hold a secret, a story waiting to be unravelled. When the final note of the music faded, and Meera ended her performance with a graceful bow, the audience erupted in applause. The sound was deafening, reverberating through the courtyard, but Meera's expression remained calm and serene, a soft smile playing on her lips. Aarav stood transfixed, still caught in the spell of her dance. Something deep inside him shifted at that moment – a sense of connection that defied logic.

As the crowd began to disperse, Aarav's colleague turned to him with a grin. "Incredible, isn't she? They say she's been trained by the finest gurus in the country. Her family's a big deal too – old money, very traditional. But she's more than just a dancer. She's... magic." "Magic," Aarav murmured, his eyes still following Meera as she gracefully navigated through the throng of admirers, her poise unwavering. Yes, that was the word. There was something almost otherworldly about her presence, a magnetism that went beyond beauty or talent. He had to meet her, even if just to say a few words. With a mix of nerves and excitement, Aarav made his way through the crowd, each step measured and deliberate.

As he approached, he noticed the subtle shift in the atmosphere around her – people parted respectfully, offering her space yet constantly vying for her attention. But Meera seemed untouched by it all, as if her mind were elsewhere. "Excuse me, Miss Kapoor," Aarav ventured softly, his voice almost lost amidst the chattering of the crowd. Meera turned, her gaze landing on him with a calm, curious intensity that made his heart stutter. "Yes?" Her voice was low and melodious, holding a quiet strength. "I-" Aarav hesitated, suddenly feeling foolish. What was he doing, approaching a woman of her stature like this? "I just wanted to say your performance was... mesmerising. I've never seen anything like it." There was a moment of silence, then Meera's smile softened, genuine. "Thank you. It's always wonderful to know that my dance speaks to people."

Her humility caught him off guard. She didn't seem like someone weighed down by the privilege and expectations that came with her family name. There was an openness in her gaze, a glimmer of something untamed beneath the surface. Before Aarav could respond, a stern voice cut through the murmur of the crowd. "Meera, it's time to go." A tall man in his late fifties stood a few paces away, his posture commanding. Mr. Kapoor. Aarav had heard of him—one of the city's influential figures, known for his strict adherence to tradition. His eyes flicked to Aarav, and something cold and assessing passed through his gaze. Meera's smile faded slightly, but she inclined her head. "Yes, father."

With a quick nod to Aarav, she turned and followed Mr. Kapoor, leaving Aarav standing amidst the dispersing crowd, a myriad of emotions swirling within him. Disappointment, confusion, and – was that hope? He didn't know what had just happened, but he knew one thing for sure: this wasn't the end. Somehow, he was going to see her again.

Chapter 2

Storm Clouds Gather

The monsoon rains continued their relentless onslaught, drenching Bombay in an endless torrent. The city seemed to blur at the edges, softened by the downpour. Yet, beneath the surface, life thrummed with a feverish intensity, as if the rain itself had infused every corner with an urgency that defied the sluggishness of the waterlogged streets. In the days following her mesmerising performance, Meera Kapoor found herself caught in a whirlwind of conflicting emotions. Her routine continued as always – morning rehearsals at the studio, afternoons spent at cultural events, and evenings filled with family obligations. But something had changed. Despite her best efforts, she couldn't erase the memory of a pair of earnest eyes watching her from the crowd that night. The thought of Aarav Deshmukh lingered like an uninvited guest, shadowing her every step.

She had met many admirers over the years. Men who flattered her with flowery words, hoping to catch a glimpse of the enigma behind the elegant façade. Yet, Aarav's presence had felt different. There was something disarming about his quiet sincerity, the way he looked at her—not just with admiration, but as if he saw through the layers of grace and poise to the person beneath. Still, Meera knew better than to dwell on such thoughts. Her life had been planned out meticulously; each decision weighed and measured. She was the daughter of Mr. Kapoor, after all—a man whose name commanded respect and fear in equal measure. For as long as she could remember, her father's words had been law. He was a figure of authority, an unyielding force in her life who had shaped her path with an iron hand.

But as the days turned into weeks, she couldn't deny the restlessness stirring within her. Aarav had sought her out twice since that fateful night, and each encounter had been brief but intense. The way his eyes lit up when he saw her, the way he seemed genuinely interested in her thoughts and dreams—it was unsettling. And exhilarating. Tonight, however, there was no room for personal musings. The Kapoor household was abuzz with activity, a subtle yet unmistakable undercurrent of tension humming through the air. Meera's father had called for a family meeting, a rare occurrence that sent ripples of apprehension through the mansion. Mr. Kapoor was not a man given to trivialities. If he had something to say, it was of utmost importance.

Meera's mother, graceful and composed as ever, busied herself with preparing the drawing room. The servants moved quickly, lighting incense sticks, arranging cushions, and setting out trays of snacks and tea. The soft glow of the chandelier bathed the room in a warm, inviting light, but to Meera, it felt more like the stage for an impending confrontation. "Do you know what this is about?" Meera whispered to her mother, who adjusted a vase of fresh flowers, her fingers trembling ever so slightly. Her mother paused; her eyes shadowed with concern. "Your father didn't say. But I have a feeling..." She trailed off, casting a furtive glance toward the doorway. "Just... be calm, Meera. Whatever happens, stay calm." Before Meera could respond, the heavy thud of footsteps echoed down the hallway. Mr. Kapoor entered, his presence filling the room like a sudden gust of wind. He was dressed in his customary white kurta-pyjama, his silver hair combed back neatly, his expression stern.

"Sit down," he ordered, his gaze sweeping over Meera and her mother. They complied, taking their places on the plush sofas. Mr. Kapoor remained standing, his posture rigid, hands clasped behind his back. He looked at Meera with an intensity that made her feel small, like a child caught doing something she shouldn't. "There are matters we need to discuss," he began, his voice low but commanding. "The time has come for us to think seriously about your future, Meera. You're not a child anymore. You've accomplished much with your dancing, and I'm proud of you for that. But there are other responsibilities that come with being a Kapoor." A cold shiver ran down Meera's spine. She knew where this conversation was heading, and it made her heart race with a mix of dread and defiance.

"Father, I—"

"Let me finish," he interrupted sharply, silencing her. "You must understand that as my daughter, your choices reflect on this family. I have started receiving inquiries—proposals, from families of good standing. Families who would be suitable matches for you." Meera's heart sank. There it was—the cage, closing in around her. She had known this day would come, but she had always hoped for more time. More freedom. Her gaze shifted to her mother, who looked down, avoiding eye contact. "I've arranged a meeting with one such family," Mr. Kapoor continued, his tone brooking no argument. "They are well-respected, and their son is educated and accomplished—a good match in every sense. We will host them tomorrow evening." "Tomorrow?" Meera's voice was barely a whisper, a tremor of disbelief running through it.

"Yes, tomorrow." Mr. Kapoor's eyes narrowed. "This is not a discussion, Meera. You will be present, and you will conduct yourself with the dignity and respect befitting a Kapoor." For a moment, the room was deathly silent. Meera's thoughts churned wildly, a storm of emotions swirling within her—anger, fear, frustration. How could her father make such decisions for her so casually, as if her life were nothing more than a business transaction? But she knew better than to argue. Mr. Kapoor was not a man who tolerated defiance. To challenge him would be to invite a confrontation she wasn't prepared for. So, instead, she forced herself to nod, lowering her gaze to hide the rebellion simmering beneath. "Yes, father," she murmured, the words bitter on her tongue.

The tension in the room seemed to ease slightly, and Mr. Kapoor's expression softened, if only a fraction. "Good. That's settled, then. I expect you to be at your best tomorrow. No distractions, no excuses." With that, he turned and left the room, leaving a suffocating silence in his wake. Meera's mother reached out, placing a gentle hand on her shoulder. "Meera..." "I'm fine," Meera said, her voice tight. "I just... need some time to think." Before her mother could respond, Meera stood and walked briskly out of the room. She felt like she was suffocating, the walls of the mansion closing in on her. She needed space—air. As she stepped onto the balcony, the cool rain-laden breeze brushed against her face, soothing the turmoil within her. She gripped the railing tightly, her knuckles white, and closed her eyes.

What was she going to do? The thought of meeting a stranger, of being evaluated like some prized possession, made her stomach turn. And then there was Aarav. She barely knew him, yet the thought of never seeing him again filled her with a deep, inexplicable sorrow. Could she defy her father? Could she risk everything—her family's honour, her own future—just for the chance to follow her heart? She didn't know. But she knew one thing for certain: tomorrow evening would change everything. And with that realisation came a new, terrifying clarity.

This was just the beginning of a storm – a storm that threatened to shatter everything she had ever known.

Chapter 3

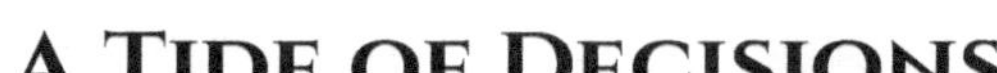

A Tide of Decisions

The following day dawned heavy and grey; the sky laden with thick clouds that seemed ready to burst at any moment. Bombay's monsoon had yet to ease its grip on the city, and the unrelenting rain created a drumming soundtrack to the unease simmering within the Kapoor household. Meera moved through her morning routine mechanically, her mind far away from the dance studio where she practised. The thud of her bare feet against the wooden floorboards echoed in the empty hall, each movement perfectly executed yet devoid of life. Even her instructor, accustomed to Meera's enthusiastic intensity, noticed the shift. "Enough for today, Meera," the elderly woman said gently, breaking Meera's rhythm. "Your heart isn't in it. Go home and rest."

Meera nodded, bowing respectfully before retreating from the studio, her thoughts tangled and tumultuous. As she stepped out into the misty drizzle, the air was cool and fresh, the scent of wet earth grounding her. But nothing could calm the storm raging within. Tonight, her father would present her to a prospective suitor—a man she'd never met, never spoken to. The sheer injustice of it boiled beneath her composed façade, threatening to spill over. Her whole life had been carefully choreographed by her father's will, each step dictated by his expectations. And now, when she had finally glimpsed something—someone—beyond that rigid framework, the walls were closing in on her once more.

Aarav's face flashed through her mind, his eyes sincere and unwavering. Their conversations, brief and scattered as they were, had left a mark on her heart. He had looked at her as no one else had before—without judgement, without preconceived notions. He had seen her, truly seen her, and the thought of losing that connection, of never seeing him again, was unbearable. Desperation clawed at her chest. She couldn't simply acquiesce to her father's wishes. But what choice did she have? Defying Mr. Kapoor was unthinkable. The repercussions would ripple far beyond her own life, staining her family's honour and fracturing the delicate balance of power and respect they held within the community.

As she wandered aimlessly through the city, the rain soaking through her light shawl, she found herself standing outside a familiar café. The quaint, sea-facing establishment had become a sanctuary of sorts for her and Aarav, a place where they could exist outside the constraints of tradition and obligation. Taking a deep breath, Meera pushed open the door and stepped inside. The bell above the entrance chimed softly, announcing her presence. She scanned the room, her heart sinking slightly when she didn't spot him. But just as she was about to turn away, a quiet voice called out from a corner booth. "Meera?" Her head snapped up, eyes widening as she saw Aarav rising from his seat, surprise and concern etched across his face. "Aarav..." She hadn't meant to find him here, but seeing him now felt like a lifeline thrown to a drowning soul.

"What are you doing here?" he asked softly, stepping closer. His presence was a comforting warmth amidst the cold, dreary atmosphere of the café. "You look... troubled." Meera hesitated, her gaze flicking around the small, dimly lit space. The few patrons were absorbed in their own worlds, paying no attention to them. "I—" The words caught in her throat, the enormity of her situation weighing heavily on her shoulders. "I didn't know where else to go." "Come," Aarav murmured, gesturing to the corner table. "Sit down. Talk to me." Slowly, almost reluctantly, she allowed him to guide her to the secluded nook. They sat across from each other, the quiet intimacy of the moment wrapping around them like a cocoon. Aarav's dark eyes searched her face, his expression pensive.

"What's wrong?" he asked softly. "Something's happened, hasn't it?" Meera took a deep, shaky breath, her fingers twisting the edge of her shawl. "My father," she began, the words coming out haltingly. "He's arranged a meeting tonight. With a family... to discuss a marriage proposal." Aarav's face tightened, his jaw clenching slightly. "A marriage proposal?" The disbelief and hurt in his voice cut through her like a knife. "So soon?" She nodded miserably. "He's been planning it for a while, I think. But it's happening now. Tonight. I'm supposed to meet them, to... to show myself as the dutiful daughter, the perfect bride-to-be."

Silence fell between them, heavy and suffocating. Aarav stared at her, the emotions flickering across his face—shock, anger, and something deeper, more desperate. "And what about what you want, Meera?" he demanded quietly, his voice taut. "Doesn't your father care about that?" "Of course not." The bitterness in her tone surprised even her. "To him, my wants don't matter. Only the family's reputation does." Aarav leaned forward; his eyes boring into hers. "So, what will you do? Are you going to let him decide your future, just like that?" The question hung between them, a challenge and a plea all at once. Meera swallowed hard, feeling tears prick at the back of her eyes. "What can I do, Aarav? I'm trapped. If I refuse, if I defy him... it will destroy everything."

"Then come with me," Aarav said suddenly, the intensity in his voice startling her. "Leave all of this behind. We'll go somewhere far away, somewhere your father's reach can't touch us. We'll start over, just you and me." Meera stared at him, her heart pounding wildly. Was he serious? Eloping— running away from her family, her life, her responsibilities— it was unthinkable. And yet, the idea sent a thrill through her, a wild, reckless hope that threatened to sweep her away. "But how?" she whispered, shaking her head in confusion. "Where would we go? How would we—" "We'll figure it out," Aarav insisted, his voice fierce. "We can leave tonight, before your meeting. We'll find a train, a bus—anything to get us out of this city. We'll find a way, Meera, I promise." Her heart was a tempest, torn between fear and longing. Could she really do it? Could she walk away from everything she had ever known, risk her family's wrath, just for a chance at freedom—at love?

"I..." She faltered, staring at Aarav with wide, uncertain eyes. "I need to think." "There's no time," Aarav urged gently, reaching across the table to take her hands in his. His touch was warm and steady, grounding her in the midst of the chaos swirling around them. "Meera, I know it's a lot to ask. But if you stay, your father will force you into this marriage. You'll be trapped, and we'll lose each other." Tears welled in her eyes, blurring her vision. He was right. If she didn't act now, tonight, it would all be over. Her father would seal her fate, and Aarav would become nothing more than a bittersweet memory. But leaving meant tearing her world apart. It meant abandoning her mother, shaming her family, and stepping into the unknown with nothing but the hope that love would be enough.

"Okay," she whispered finally, the word trembling on her lips. "Okay, Aarav. I'll go with you." Relief and joy flooded Aarav's face, and he squeezed her hands gently. "We'll meet at the docks, by the old lighthouse. Ten o'clock. I'll be waiting for you." Meera nodded, her heart a chaotic mess of emotions. "I'll be there." As they left the café, their decision hung in the air between them, fragile and dangerous. They had chosen love, defiance, and freedom. But Bombay was a city of secrets and shadows, and fate had never been kind to those who dared to dream. Tonight, under the cover of darkness and rain, they would make their escape.

Or so they thought.

CHAPTER 4

SHADOWS OF THE PAST

The city was a blur of rain and shadows as Meera made her way through the narrow, winding lanes of South Bombay. Night had fallen, shrouding everything in a cloak of darkness, save for the occasional flicker of streetlights reflecting off the slick, rain-soaked roads. Her heart pounded in her chest as she glanced at her watch—9:45 p.m. She was cutting it close. The meeting with the suitor's family had ended just over an hour ago, but it felt like a lifetime. Meera's father had been so pleased, smiling and exchanging pleasantries with the guests. Her mother, on the other hand, had been a silent pillar of composure, though Meera could see the worry etched in her eyes. Meera had played her part flawlessly—graceful, polite, and utterly obedient. But inside, every fibre of her being had screamed to get away, to escape the suffocating mask of perfection she wore.

The suitor, Rahul Verma, had been handsome and charming, speaking politely about his career and ambitions. But Meera had barely heard a word. Her mind had been on Aarav, on the promise they had made. All through the evening, she had watched the clock, counting down the minutes until she could slip away. And now she was running—running toward freedom, toward the future she had chosen, not the one chosen for her. The docks loomed ahead, shrouded in mist and darkness. She could see the faint outline of the lighthouse in the distance, its solitary beam cutting through the night like a beacon of hope. The salty tang of the sea mixed with the scent of rain, and the sound of waves crashing against the stone pier filled her ears.

She slowed her pace as she neared the meeting spot, her eyes scanning the deserted docks anxiously. And then she saw him—standing under the shadow of the old lighthouse, his silhouette outlined by the dim glow of a distant streetlamp. Aarav. He turned at the sound of her footsteps, his face lighting up with relief as he saw her. "Meera!" he called softly, rushing toward her. "Aarav," she breathed, throwing herself into his arms. The tension, the fear, the uncertainty—all of it melted away the moment she felt his warmth. "I made it. I'm here." "I knew you would," he murmured, holding her tightly. "I knew you'd come." For a moment, they simply clung to each other, the rain soaking through their clothes, but neither of them cared. They were together, and that was all that mattered.

"We need to go," Aarav said finally, pulling back slightly to look into her eyes. "There's a train leaving from Victoria Terminus at midnight. It'll take us to Pune. From there, we can disappear—start over somewhere new." Meera nodded, swallowing hard. The enormity of what they were doing weighed heavily on her, but she pushed the fear aside. She had made her choice. She would not turn back now. "Let's go," she whispered. They turned toward the exit of the pier, but before they could take more than a few steps, a figure stepped out of the shadows, blocking their path. "Going somewhere, cousin?" Meera froze, her breath catching in her throat. The voice was low, rough around the edges, but unmistakable. Slowly, she looked up, her eyes widening as she took in the sight of the man standing before them.

"Vikram?" she whispered, her heart dropping like a stone. Vikram Kapoor stood a few feet away, his tall frame half-hidden in the gloom. His hair was damp from the rain, and his face, lean and angular, was etched with shadows. There was a flicker of something unreadable in his eyes as he looked from Meera to Aarav, his expression caught between anger and sorrow. "What are you doing here?" Meera demanded, her voice trembling. She hadn't seen Vikram in years—not since he had been cast out of the family. His sudden reappearance now, at this moment, felt like a cruel twist of fate. "I could ask you the same thing," Vikram replied, his tone cold. "Running away in the dead of night, with a stranger, no less. What are you thinking, Meera?"

"How did you find us?" Aarav asked sharply, stepping protectively in front of Meera. Vikram's gaze shifted to Aarav, narrowing slightly. "I have my ways. And Meera is still my family, no matter what she thinks." He took a step closer, his eyes boring into Meera's. "You can't do this, Meera. You can't just disappear. Think about what it will do to your parents, to the family." Meera stiffened, anger flaring in her chest. "Why do you care?" she snapped. "You haven't been a part of this family for years. Why are you suddenly so concerned?" "Because I know what happens when you defy the Kapoors," Vikram shot back, his voice sharp. "I know better than anyone. And I don't want you to make the same mistakes I did."

Silence fell, thick and heavy. Meera stared at him, her mind whirling. Vikram's presence was like a ghost from the past—a past that had been whispered about in hushed tones, never spoken of openly. Her father had forbidden anyone from mentioning Vikram's name after he had been disowned, and Meera had grown up believing him to be the black sheep of the family, a cautionary tale of what happened when you strayed from the path set for you. But now, seeing him here, his face drawn and haunted, she realised there was so much more to the story. "What are you talking about?" she asked quietly. "What mistakes?" Vikram sighed, running a hand through his wet hair. "There are things you don't know, Meera. Things your father never told you. The truth about why I was cast out."

"I don't care," Meera said fiercely. "I'm not staying. I'm not going to let father decide my life for me." "I'm not asking you to stay," Vikram said, his voice gentling. "I'm asking you to listen. Just listen, Meera. You need to know what you're walking away from." She hesitated, glancing up at Aarav. He looked tense, his jaw clenched, but he nodded slightly. "Let him speak," he murmured. Meera turned back to Vikram, crossing her arms defensively. "Fine. Talk." Vikram took a deep breath, his gaze locked on hers. "You think your father is a tyrant, that he only cares about control and reputation. And you're right, to an extent. But there's more to it than that." He paused, his expression darkening. "Years ago, I made a mistake. A mistake that almost ruined the family."

"What mistake?" Aarav asked quietly. "I got involved in a project—an investment opportunity that seemed too good to pass up," Vikram explained, his voice low. "But it turned out to be a front for something else—something illegal. By the time I realised what was happening, it was too late. Our family name was already tied to it." Meera's eyes widened. "Illegal? What do you mean?" "Money laundering," Vikram said bluntly. "And I was right in the middle of it." Shock rippled through Meera. She had never heard any of this before. Her father had always spoken of Vikram's downfall as a matter of personal disgrace, a betrayal of family values. But to be involved in something criminal...

"I tried to fix it," Vikram continued, his expression pained. "But the damage was done. The authorities were closing in, and the scandal was about to break. Father had to act fast to protect the family. He cut me off, disowned me publicly. He made me the scapegoat so that the rest of the family could remain untouched." Meera's heart twisted painfully. "He sacrificed you." "Yes," Vikram said softly. "And I accepted it. Because I knew I had to. Because I owed it to him—to all of you. But it destroyed me, Meera. It ruined my life." He looked at her with a desperate intensity. "I'm not saying this to make you pity me. I'm saying it because I don't want you to go through the same thing. If you run away tonight, if you defy father like this, he will cut you off completely. He will erase you from this family's history, just like he did to me. And you'll be alone, with nowhere to go."

Meera stared at him, her heart pounding. She glanced at Aarav, whose face was taut with shock and anger. "Is that true?" Aarav whispered. "He would really do that to you,

Meera?" "Yes," Vikram answered quietly. "He would. And it won't just end with you. Your mother, our relatives—everyone will be affected. The scandal will haunt them for years." Tears welled in Meera's eyes. What was she supposed to do? Stay and be a prisoner in her own life? Or run and lose everything she had ever known? "What do you want from me, Vikram?" she choked out. "What should I do?" "Come back," Vikram said gently. "Let's find another way. We can fight this together, Meera. I'm not asking you to give up on Aarav. I'm asking you to stay and face it with us."

Meera felt like the world was crumbling around her. Everything she thought she knew was unravelling. She looked at Aarav, silently begging him for an answer, a sign. But his eyes, filled with pain and love, held only one message: Whatever you choose, I'm with you. The storm raged around them, a fierce wind whipping at their clothes, the rain pelting down harder than ever.

At that moment, Meera realised that no matter what she chose, nothing would ever be the same again.

CHAPTER 5

ECHOES OF TRADITION

The next few weeks were a blur of decisions and plans, both painstakingly detailed and fraught with uncertainty. Meera and Aarav had made their choice: they would not run. But neither would they submit quietly to the life her father had laid out for her. Instead, they had chosen a middle path, one that neither defied nor surrendered, but rather sought to bridge the gap between tradition and individuality. It was Vikram who had planted the seed of the idea that would become their salvation. With his knowledge of the family's history and his deep understanding of the social dynamics that governed Bombay's elite circles, he had proposed something radical yet surprisingly fitting: a cultural initiative that would both honour and challenge the legacy of the Kapoor family. It would be a way to reclaim their identity, not by rejecting the past, but by embracing it and reshaping it for a new era.

The project, dubbed "Echoes of Tradition," would be a multi-faceted cultural festival celebrating classical dance, music, and the arts—fields in which the Kapoor family had once been pioneers. It would acknowledge their contributions while also addressing the shadows that lingered over their name. The festival would be public, inclusive, and above all, it would offer a platform for open dialogue and healing. For Meera, the project was more than just a chance to assert her voice; it was a way to reclaim her art, her heritage, and her autonomy. With Aarav and Vikram by her side, she threw herself into the preparations, channelling all her conflicting emotions into a flurry of creative activity. But there were moments of doubt; moments when she wondered if they were deluding themselves, trying to fight against a tide that could not be turned.

Mr. Kapoor, initially furious when Meera had refused the engagement and presented the idea of the festival, had reacted with cold, simmering silence. For days, he refused to speak to her, his stern disapproval hanging over the household like a dark cloud. But as word of the initiative began to spread and support started trickling in from unexpected quarters, his resistance wavered. Even the most rigid traditionalists were intrigued by the proposal, seeing in it a potential resurgence of the family's status as cultural patrons. The festival planning took on a life of its own. Meera, Aarav, and Vikram worked tirelessly, their energy feeding off one another in a complex dance of hope, fear, and determination. Aarav's role as a partner in the venture cemented his place not only in Meera's life but also, subtly, within the family's sphere. He became involved in every aspect of the project, from coordinating with local artists to managing logistics and technology. His background in software engineering gave the initiative a modern edge, blending technology with tradition in a way that was fresh and compelling.

Vikram, on the other hand, used his connections to bring in high-profile supporters, people who still remembered the Kapoor family's contributions to Bombay's cultural landscape. Each new ally added weight to their cause, slowly chipping away at the stigma that had lingered for years. But for Meera, the real test was yet to come.

The day of the festival arrived.

The air buzzed with anticipation as the sun dipped below the horizon, casting the city in a golden glow. The courtyard of the Kapoor mansion had been transformed into a grand open-air theatre, with strings of fairy lights twinkling overhead and vibrant banners fluttering in the evening breeze. Rows of seats fanned out in front of the stage, and a soft murmur of voices filled the air as guests began to arrive. The first performance of the evening was set to be Meera's— an intricate Bharatanatyam piece that she had choreographed herself, blending traditional rhythms with modern motifs. It was her statement, her declaration of independence and identity. But as she stood backstage, her heart hammering in her chest, she couldn't help but feel a surge of nerves. What if it wasn't enough? What if the audience, and more importantly, her father, rejected her efforts?

"Hey," a soft voice murmured beside her. She turned to see Aarav standing there, his eyes warm and steady. "You're going to be amazing. Just breathe." She nodded, taking a deep breath, trying to centre herself. But her hands still shook slightly as she adjusted her costume, the gold and crimson silk rustling softly. "I wish I could say I'm not nervous," she whispered, biting her lip. "You're not alone, Meera," Aarav said quietly, reaching out to squeeze her hand gently. "You have all of us behind you. And you have your art. No one can take that away." A small, grateful smile tugged at her lips. "Thank you, Aarav. For everything." Before she could say more, the sound of the announcer's voice rang out, and a hush fell over the crowd. "Ladies and gentlemen, welcome to the first evening of 'Echoes of Tradition,' a celebration of our city's rich cultural heritage and the legacy of the Kapoor family. To open tonight's festivities, we have a special performance by none other than Meera Kapoor, who will be presenting a new piece dedicated to the fusion of past and present. Please welcome her to the stage."

The applause that followed was polite, but cautious—curious. Meera knew the stakes were high. This wasn't just a dance; it was a statement of intent. Squaring her shoulders, she took a deep breath and stepped out onto the stage. The lights were dazzling, the sea of faces blurring into the darkness beyond. But as the first notes of the music filled the air, something shifted inside her. The fear and doubt melted away, replaced by a fierce, quiet resolve. She began to move. Her body flowed through the complex patterns of the choreography, each gesture precise yet fluid. Her feet struck the stage in a staccato rhythm, the bells around her ankles ringing out like a heartbeat. She spun, leapt, and swayed, her movements a perfect blend of control and abandon. And as the dance progressed, she wove in elements that were new—unexpected. Contemporary nuances, seamlessly blended with the grace of classical forms, added a fresh and distinctive rhythm to the performance. It was a dance that spoke of evolution, of a tradition that was not stagnant but alive, growing, and changing.

The audience leaned forward, caught between surprise and admiration. And then, slowly, the applause began to build, hesitant at first, then gaining strength as the audience recognised what they were seeing: a bridge between the old and the new, a celebration that honoured the past without being confined by it. When the final note faded, and Meera sank to her knees in a graceful bow, the courtyard erupted in cheers. The sound washed over her, filling her with a heady rush of relief and triumph. She rose slowly, breathing hard, and looked out into the crowd. And there, standing at the very edge of the audience, was her father. Mr. Kapoor's face was unreadable, his expression a mask of stern composure. But there was something in his eyes, a flicker of emotion so fleeting she almost missed it. He held her gaze for a long, tense moment, then inclined his head ever so slightly.

It wasn't approval. But it wasn't rejection, either. It was... acknowledgement. A tear slipped down Meera's cheek, unbidden. She bowed again, deeper this time, and then turned and left the stage. Backstage, Aarav and Vikram were waiting, their faces alight with pride and joy. Vikram pulled her into a tight hug, murmuring words of praise and encouragement, while Aarav stood back, his eyes shining. "You did it, Meera," Aarav said softly. "You did it." "No," she whispered, shaking her head as she looked between them, at the people who had stood by her through it all. "We did it." As the night wore on and the festival continued with performances from other artists, the mood in the courtyard shifted. Guests who had been sceptical began to relax, their interest piqued, their respect rekindled. They spoke of the Kapoor family's contribution to the arts, of Meera's courage and talent.

The whispers of disapproval were drowned out by words of admiration and hope. By the time the evening drew to a close, "Echoes of Tradition" was no longer just a festival—it was a new beginning. As Meera stood beside Aarav and Vikram, watching the lights of the stage fade into the misty night, she knew that they had done more than just reclaim the Kapoor name. They had carved out a space for themselves, a place where love and tradition, past and present, could coexist.

For the first time in her life, Meera felt free.

CHAPTER 6

A STORM RECLAIMED

Months had passed since the night that had changed everything—the night when the Kapoor family's narrative began to transform from a legacy of rigid tradition to a story of reconciliation and evolution. The success of the "Echoes of Tradition" initiative had rippled through the community, sparking conversations that went beyond the immediate drama of Meera's defiance and Aarav's presence. It had reignited an appreciation for heritage while paving the way for modern interpretations, and, most importantly, it had allowed the Kapoors to face the shadows of their past without shame. Meera stood on the balcony of her home, gazing out at the sprawling cityscape of Bombay. The monsoon rains had returned, washing over the city in silvery sheets, painting the skyline in shades of misty grey and emerald green. But this time, the rain didn't feel like a harbinger of turmoil. It felt cleansing, like a promise of renewal.

She had changed since that stormy night at the docks. She was no longer just the dutiful daughter of Mr. Kapoor, the flawless dancer who performed her art according to others' expectations. She was something more now—an artist, a pioneer, and a woman who had claimed her own identity amidst the swirling chaos of tradition and rebellion. And she had not done it alone. A soft knock on the balcony door made her turn. Aarav stepped out, his presence immediately warming the damp chill of the evening. He wore a loose kurta, his hair tousled from the wind. His smile, gentle and knowing, was the same one that had pulled her back from the brink of despair so many times.

"Lost in thought again?" he teased lightly, coming to stand beside her. Meera smiled, leaning into him as his arm wrapped around her shoulders. "Always," she murmured. "There's so much to think about." "Good things, I hope." "Yes," she said softly, glancing up at him. "Mostly good things. But also... complicated things." His brow furrowed slightly. "What kind of complicated things?" "Us," she replied, her voice barely audible above the soft patter of rain. "Our future. My family. Everything we're trying to build." Aarav's expression softened. He turned, cupping her face gently in his hands. "We've made it this far, haven't we? Through the anger, the rejection, the disapproval... And look where we are now."

Where they were, indeed. The initiative they had started had blossomed into something much larger than they'd anticipated. "Echoes of Tradition" was no longer just a one-time festival; it had become a movement. Communities across Bombay—and beyond—were embracing the idea of merging tradition with modernity, of using art and culture as a means of bridging generational divides. Meera and Aarav had become the unofficial ambassadors of this cause, their partnership serving as a living example of what it meant to challenge norms without shattering them.

But it hadn't been easy. There had been setbacks and opposition—angry letters, subtle threats, and even public confrontations. Mr. Kapoor's acceptance of their endeavour had been slow and begrudging. Though he had softened toward Aarav, there were still moments when the old barriers reasserted themselves, and the tensions between father and daughter flared anew. Yet, each time, Meera had stood firm. And each time, Aarav had been there, steady and unwavering. "Your father sees it now," Aarav continued quietly. "He may not say it outright, but he understands what we're doing—what you're doing. He's proud of you, Meera." "Is he?" she whispered, uncertainty shadowing her eyes.

"I think so," Aarav said softly. "And even if he isn't ready to admit it, everyone else can see it. You're changing things, Meera. You've made them see that tradition doesn't have to mean stagnation. It can grow and evolve. You've made space for something new." Meera's gaze drifted back out over the rain-drenched city. Yes, there had been progress. But one lingering question gnawed at her heart, keeping her awake at night. Was there truly a place for Aarav within this world they were creating? Or was he still an outsider—a man forever marked by his modern ideals, whose very presence challenged the traditional norms that were so deeply ingrained in her family? As if sensing her thoughts, Aarav's hold tightened. "Stop worrying," he murmured. "Whatever happens, we'll face it together. We always have."

Before Meera could respond, the sound of a throat being cleared made them both turn. Standing in the doorway, looking slightly uncomfortable and utterly out of place in the intimacy of the moment, was Mr. Kapoor. "Father,"

Meera breathed, straightening instinctively. Aarav moved back, giving them space, though he remained close enough to lend silent support. Mr. Kapoor's gaze shifted between them, lingering on their intertwined hands. Something flickered in his eyes, something complex and unreadable. "I need to speak with you," he said finally, his voice gruff but not unkind. "Both of you." Meera felt her heart jump into her throat. They had spoken so little, father and daughter, since that night. Despite the tentative peace that had settled over the household, there was still an unspoken chasm between them, a gulf of unhealed wounds and unvoiced words.

"Yes, father," she said quietly. "Of course." Mr. Kapoor hesitated, his gaze locking on Meera's. Then, slowly, he turned and gestured toward the drawing room. "Come." They followed him inside, the warmth of the house a stark contrast to the cool dampness of the balcony. The drawing room, filled with bookshelves and heirlooms from generations past, seemed both familiar and foreign. This was where so many pivotal moments in Meera's life had unfolded. Where her father had laid out her path, where decisions had been made for her without her consent. But tonight, it felt different. Tonight, it felt like a place where decisions could be made with her. Mr. Kapoor settled into his chair, his expression uncharacteristically tense. Meera and Aarav sat across from him, their hands still loosely linked.

For a long moment, no one spoke. The rain outside filled the silence, a soothing backdrop to the charged atmosphere. "I've been thinking," Mr. Kapoor began slowly, his gaze fixed on Meera. "About what you said. About what you've done." Meera held her breath, waiting. "You defied me," he continued, his voice low. "You went against everything I taught you, everything I believed in. You chose a path that I would never have chosen for you. And yet..." He trailed off, shaking his head slightly as if in disbelief. "And yet, you have succeeded. More than I ever imagined." Meera blinked, her heart pounding. Was this... praise? Coming from him?

"The festival, the initiative, the... respect you have earned for this family," Mr. Kapoor went on. "I never thought I would say this, but... you have made me see things differently. Perhaps... perhaps I have been wrong. Not in everything," he added quickly, his gaze sharpening. "But in some things." Tears stung Meera's eyes, but she forced herself to remain composed. "Father..." "I am not saying I approve of all your choices," he continued, his gaze shifting to Aarav. "But I see now that there is value in... adaptation. In compromise." He turned back to Meera, his expression softening. "If this is the life you want—if this is the man you want beside you—then so be it. But you must understand, Meera, that there will still be challenges. There will still be those who resist, who will try to undermine what you have built. It will not be easy."

"It never has been," Meera said softly, meeting his gaze. "But that doesn't mean it's not worth fighting for." Mr. Kapoor looked at her for a long time, something like pride shining faintly in his eyes. Then, slowly, he nodded. "Very well. Then fight for it. Show them that you can succeed—not because you are my daughter, but because you are... yourself." It was the closest thing to an apology—and a blessing—that Meera would ever receive. And it was enough. "Thank you," she whispered, her voice thick with emotion. Mr. Kapoor inclined his head. Then, without another word, he rose and left the room, leaving Meera and Aarav alone in the fading glow of the firelight. For a moment, they sat in silence, the enormity of what had just happened washing over them.

"Did that just—" Aarav began, his voice hoarse. "Yes," Meera murmured, a soft, incredulous laugh bubbling up inside her. "Yes, I think it did." Aarav shook his head, then leaned in and kissed her gently, his lips brushing against hers in a caress that spoke of hope, of triumph, and of a future that was finally theirs. "You did it," he whispered. "You changed his mind." "No," Meera said softly, smiling against his lips. "We did it. Together." And as the storm raged outside, the two of them held on to each other, secure in the knowledge that they had weathered the worst of it. Whatever came next, whatever challenges lay ahead, they would face them as partners, as equals, as a new kind of family.

Their story, once forbidden and fraught with turmoil, had become a testament to the power of love, resilience, and the courage to redefine tradition. It was a story that would continue to unfold, chapter by chapter, with each new dawn.

But for now, it was enough.

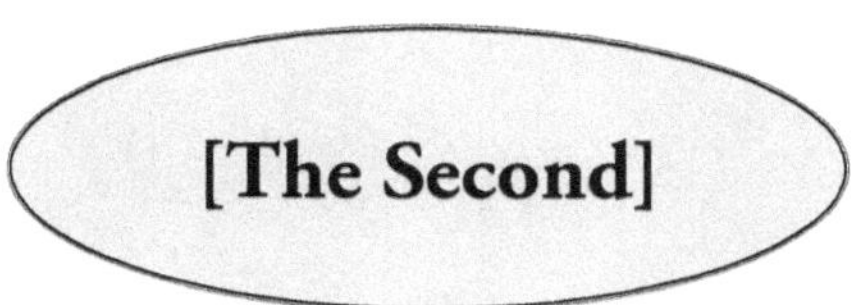

The Reunion of Hearts

CHAPTER 1

ECHOES OF ST. JOHN'S

The evening sky over Mumbai was a canvas of fading blue and warm orange, as the sun dipped behind the city skyline. A light mist hung in the air, leftover from the recent monsoon rains, and the scent of damp earth mingled with the vibrant aroma of street vendors cooking fresh snacks for the evening crowd. Maverick breathed in deeply, letting the familiar scents of his childhood home seep into his bones. After so many years, Mumbai still felt like a living, breathing entity—always pulsing, always changing, yet comfortingly familiar. He gazed ahead, taking in the sight of his alma mater: St. John the Evangelist High School.

With its towering Gothic architecture and sprawling ivy, the school stood as timeless as ever. Tricolour flags hung from every corner, swaying gently in the breeze, a reminder of the Independence Day celebrations that had just taken place. Maverick stood at the gates for a moment, hesitating as a wave of nostalgia hit him, mixed with a flutter of anxiety that left his heart pounding. This was his old stomping ground, yet it felt intimidating in a way he couldn't quite place. He adjusted his collar and took a deep breath. He was here for the reunion—a much-anticipated event that brought together the Class of 1993, celebrating over twenty years since they'd last walked these halls as carefree teenagers.

When the invitation had arrived a month ago, he'd almost tossed it away. His life as an architect was busy, with projects lined up in multiple cities and little time for social gatherings. But when he'd read through the names on the list of attendees, a single name had leapt out at him: Smita Patil. The name alone had transported him back to his teenage years, stirring emotions he thought he'd left behind. Smita had been his best friend, his confidante, and, though he'd never told her, his first love. But she had left suddenly, without much explanation, and he'd never quite managed to close that chapter in his life. Now, decades later, he would finally get the chance to see her again.

But the questions in his mind remained: Would Smita remember him as he remembered her? Would she recognise the unspoken bond they had shared all those years ago? Or had time erased all that they'd once meant to each other? As he walked through the gates, memories surged, enveloping him like the humidity that clung to the Mumbai air. The sound of laughter, the faint scent of chalk dust, the creaking of old doors—it all came back to him vividly. He passed by the classroom where he and Smita had sat together, laughing over inside jokes and scribbling notes that only they could decipher. Every corner held a memory, a fragment of a time when life felt simpler yet somehow richer. He didn't have to walk far before he heard a familiar voice.

"Mave! Is that you?" A figure came striding toward him with an easy, confident gait. It was Zeph—his best friend, his partner in crime, and the one person who had been by his side through every mischievous prank and daring escapade they'd managed to pull off in high school. Now a successful businessman with a booming laugh and an infectious energy, Zeph looked much the same, though with a bit more polish and a touch of grey at the temples. Maverick's face broke into a wide smile, and he braced himself as Zeph enveloped him in a bear hug, nearly knocking the air out of his lungs. "Maverick, my man! Still with that serious face, I see," Zeph teased, thumping him on the back.

"Some things never change," Maverick replied, grinning. "Though it seems like you haven't changed much either, Zeph." They spent a few minutes catching up, reminiscing about the pranks they'd pulled, the teachers they'd tormented, and the countless memories that had bound them as friends. Zeph's laughter was contagious, and for a while, Maverick's anxiety melted away. But as they chatted, his gaze kept drifting toward the entrance to the main hall, searching for a familiar face, a glimpse of the one person he'd come hoping to see. Zeph noticed the direction of his gaze and grinned knowingly. "Looking for someone, are we?" he said with a wink. "Let me guess… Smita?" Maverick felt his cheeks warm, and he chuckled, trying to brush it off. "Is it that obvious?"

"To me, it is," Zeph said, his voice softer now. "I remember how you used to look at her. I always thought you two would end up together, you know?" "Me too," Maverick replied, his voice tinged with a mix of nostalgia and regret. He wanted to explain more, but even after all these years, the words felt too personal, too raw. "But she left so suddenly. I never got the chance to tell her how I felt." Zeph nodded, his expression thoughtful. "Well, maybe tonight is your second chance, my friend. Don't let it slip away this time." Maverick gave him a grateful smile, silently appreciating his friend's support. Zeph slapped him on the back once more before disappearing into the crowd, leaving Maverick to gather his thoughts. He continued through the throng of former classmates, exchanging brief pleasantries here and there, his mind only half-focused on the conversations around him.

Then, as if drawn by fate, his eyes landed on her. Smita stood across the hall, surrounded by a small group of friends. Time seemed to slow as Maverick took in the sight of her. She was still so unmistakably Smita—the same girl he had known all those years ago, yet now, there was an air of sophistication about her. Her long, wavy hair framed her face, and her warm smile lit up her deep brown eyes. She looked radiant, confident, and every bit as captivating as he remembered. Maverick's breath caught in his throat. He could feel his pulse racing, his mind flashing back to memories that had grown hazy with time yet still felt vivid in his heart. He remembered her laugh; the way she could make him feel like he was the only person in the world who mattered when she looked at him. And for a moment, he was transported back to 1992, to the last day they'd been together, the day he had been too afraid to tell her how he felt.

But now, here she was, just a few steps away, and this time, he knew he couldn't let the moment slip away. Taking a deep breath, he moved through the crowd toward her, each step feeling like a leap into the unknown. She turned, her gaze falling on him, and her eyes widened with recognition. A slow smile spread across her face, and Maverick felt his heart leap. "Maverick?" Her voice was soft, familiar, and filled with a warmth that immediately put him at ease. She stepped closer, her gaze flickering over him as if trying to take in all the years that had passed. "I can't believe it's you." "Hi, Smita," he replied, his voice catching slightly as emotions surged within him. "It's been a long time." They embraced, the years melting away as they held onto each other for a moment, their connection rekindling as if no time had passed. As they pulled apart, Maverick could see the same spark in her eyes, a spark that made him feel like he was sixteen again, filled with the thrill of something new and beautiful.

They began to talk, catching up on the years that had passed, filling each other in on careers, travels, and the lives they had led since they had last seen each other. Maverick learned that Smita had become a well-regarded writer, her novels known for their emotional depth and poignant storytelling. She spoke about her work with pride and humility, and her passion for writing was evident in every word. In turn, Smita listened intently as Maverick described his life as an architect, his drive to create spaces that connected people with history and emotion. He could see that she was genuinely interested, her questions thoughtful, and her smile encouraged him to share more.

As the evening wore on, they decided to take a walk around the school, revisiting the places they had spent so much time in. They walked through the library where they had huddled over shared books, the classroom where they had passed notes, and the courtyard where they had laughed together under the warm sun. Each location brought a flood of memories, and they found themselves slipping back into their easy friendship, laughing and sharing as if they were still teenagers. But beneath the laughter and reminiscing, there was an undercurrent of tension, a shared awareness that there was something between them left unspoken, something that had lingered all these years, waiting to be acknowledged.

As the evening wound down, they found themselves on the rooftop of the school, overlooking the sparkling city below. The night was still, the city lights twinkling like stars. They stood side by side, silent for a moment, each lost in thought. Maverick knew that he couldn't let this moment pass. It was time to confront the feelings he had kept buried for so long. "Smita," he said, his voice barely more than a whisper. She turned to him, her gaze steady and expectant. Maverick took a deep breath, summoning the courage that had eluded him for so long.

This was his moment, and he wasn't going to let it slip away.

CHAPTER 2

THE GHOSTS WE CARRY

The rooftop was quiet except for the faint hum of the city below. Maverick looked out over Mumbai's landscape, the familiar city lights forming a shimmering constellation that stretched endlessly into the distance. The breeze brushed gently against his face, cooling his nerves as he prepared to say what had been buried inside him for over two decades. "Smita…" he began, his voice tentative. "I've thought about this moment for so many years. There were things I never got to tell you back then, things I never had the courage to say." He glanced at her, and she was watching him with an openness that made him feel vulnerable yet safe. Her expression was a blend of curiosity and empathy, as if she sensed the weight of his words even before he spoke them.

"What is it, Maverick?" Her voice was soft, encouraging. She took a step closer, her eyes reflecting a deep understanding he hadn't realised he had missed so much. He suddenly felt the years fall away, the responsibilities, the career, the life he'd built, and he was just Maverick, the boy who had once been in awe of the girl standing beside him. He took a breath, steadying himself. "Back in school, you were everything to me," he said, his words coming out in a rush. "My best friend, my confidante… and so much more than I ever dared to admit. I always thought I'd have time to tell you, to explain how much you meant to me. But then you left, and I didn't get the chance." He could feel the weight of his confession in the air, a vulnerability that left him exposed but strangely liberated. Smita's eyes softened as she listened, and he saw her take a deep breath as if steadying herself.

"Maverick, I…" She hesitated, a shadow crossing her face, and for a moment, he saw something flicker in her gaze—a sadness, an unresolved pain that mirrored his own. She looked away, her hand resting on the railing, her fingers tracing an invisible pattern against the cool metal. "There's something I need to tell you, too," she said finally, her voice barely above a whisper. She glanced back at him, her gaze steady yet filled with an unreadable emotion. "I didn't leave because I wanted to. I left because… well, life had other plans for me." She looked out at the city lights, her face illuminated by their glow, and Maverick sensed that this moment was as difficult for her as it was for him. Smita had always been an open book with him back in school, but now, there was a guardedness about her, a layer of protection she had built around herself that hadn't been there before.

"My family… they were going through a lot back then," she continued, her voice faltering slightly. "There were things I never told you, things I tried to keep hidden. My parents were struggling, fighting over everything, and it was tearing our family apart. When my father got a job offer in another city, they thought moving would somehow solve all their problems." She paused, her voice thick with emotion.

"Leaving St. John's wasn't my choice. If I'd had any say, I would have stayed. I would have fought to be here—with you." Her words hung in the air, raw and filled with the pain of choices that had been made for her. Maverick felt a surge of empathy, a new understanding of the weight she had carried alone. He had imagined countless reasons for her sudden departure, but he'd never considered that she might have been going through struggles of her own, that her silence might have been a shield to protect herself from the turmoil she'd been forced to endure.

"Smita, I… I'm so sorry," he said, his voice filled with sincerity. He reached out, covering her hand with his, and she didn't pull away. Instead, she looked at him, her eyes glistening with unshed tears, and he felt the depth of their connection, the unspoken understanding that had always bound them together. She took a shuddering breath, blinking back the tears. "Thank you, Maverick. For listening… for understanding. I never got to explain it to anyone, and over time, it felt easier to just bury it all, to pretend it was a chapter that had closed. But coming back here, seeing you again, it's… it's brought back everything I tried so hard to forget." He could see the burden of her past etched in the lines of her face, the way her shoulders slumped ever so slightly as if she had been carrying a weight for far too long. He understood now that they both had ghosts to carry, scars that had shaped them in ways neither had fully acknowledged.

As they stood there, a comfortable silence settled between them, the kind of silence that only true friends could share. For the first time in years, Maverick felt a sense of peace, as if he had finally reclaimed a part of himself that had been missing. Smita had always been his missing piece, and now, standing beside her, he felt whole again. "Do you remember that last day at school?" Smita asked, a faint smile tugging at the corners of her lips. "The day before I left?" He chuckled softly, the memory surfacing in his mind. "I remember it well. You were laughing so hard you could barely breathe, and I was convinced I was the funniest person in the world." She laughed, and the sound was warm and familiar, like an old song he had nearly forgotten. "You were," she replied. "I don't even remember what joke you told, but I remember how happy I felt, like nothing else mattered."

They fell into an easy rhythm, recounting stories of their school days, the pranks they'd pulled, the adventures they'd embarked on. Each story brought them closer, filling in the gaps of the years they'd lost, and Maverick felt the barriers between them dissolving, replaced by a trust that only time could forge. As the evening wore on, the sky darkened, and a chill settled over the rooftop. Smita wrapped her arms around herself, shivering slightly, and Maverick, without a second thought, shrugged off his jacket and draped it over her shoulders. She looked up at him, her eyes warm with gratitude, and for a moment, he felt a glimmer of the boy he had once been, the boy who would have done anything to see her smile. "Maverick, I want to know..." she said softly, her voice barely above a whisper. "Why did you come tonight? After all these years, why now?"

He felt his heart skip a beat, her question catching him off guard. But he knew there was no point in holding back. Not now, not when they had come this far. "Because I never stopped thinking about you," he admitted, his voice raw and unguarded. "I wanted closure, maybe even a second chance. To be honest, I wasn't sure what I was looking for when I walked through those gates tonight. But now, I realise that I was searching for you. For the part of me that I left behind when you disappeared from my life." She looked at him, her eyes soft with a mixture of surprise and something deeper, something he had dared to hope for but never expected to see. The space between them seemed to shrink, and he felt his heart pounding, anticipation and vulnerability mingling within him. But just as he opened his mouth to say more, a voice interrupted them.

"Smita! Maverick! We're all heading out for drinks. You guys coming?" It was Zeph, his tone jovial, and they turned to see him grinning at them from the doorway. Smita glanced at Maverick, her smile a mix of apology and regret. "Maybe we should join them," she said, though her gaze lingered on him, as if reluctant to leave the intimate space they had created. Maverick gave a small nod, suppressing the disappointment that flared within him. "Yeah, let's go." They followed Zeph down the stairs, back to the main hall where their classmates were gathering, laughing and making plans to continue the evening. As they rejoined the group, the spell between them seemed to fade, replaced by the noise and energy of the reunion. But Maverick couldn't shake the feeling that something had shifted, that their bond had deepened in ways he hadn't anticipated.

As they joined the others, Maverick caught Smita's gaze, and she gave him a small smile, a silent promise that their conversation wasn't over—that their story, after all these years, was only just beginning.

CHAPTER 3

PATHS CROSSED AND DIVIDED

The reunion after-party was held in a lively café on the city's edge, with a sprawling terrace that overlooked the restless ocean. Maverick's friends filled the space, their laughter blending with the crashing waves below. But amid the conversations and clinking glasses, his attention kept drifting back to Smita. She was laughing with their old friends, her smile as radiant as he remembered, but he could sense an underlying tension, a weight that hadn't been there in their school days. He turned his glass in his hand, contemplating her words from earlier, the confessions they had both made. In the years they'd been apart, he'd always wondered what his life might have been like if he'd confessed his feelings back then, if they had dared to explore something more. Instead, he'd let the chance slip away, waiting for the "right time" that never came.

"Still the introspective one, aren't you?" A familiar voice broke through his thoughts. He looked up to see Shalini, an old friend from their group, grinning at him. Shalini had been the class prankster, always with a witty comeback and quick to bring a smile to anyone's face. "Maybe," Maverick replied with a small smile. "Some things never change." She raised an eyebrow, glancing over her shoulder at Smita, who was engaged in conversation on the far side of the terrace. "I always thought you and Smita had some unfinished business. Looks like I was right." "Shalini…" Maverick hesitated, unsure how much he wanted to share. But she had always been perceptive, the kind of friend who could read him even when he tried to hide his emotions. He sighed, leaning against the terrace railing. "I didn't expect to see her again. And now that I have, I feel like I'm being pulled in two directions. There's a part of me that wants to just… dive back in and pick up where we left off. But I'm not that naive kid anymore. Life has changed me. I've changed."

Shalini nodded, her smile softening. "And maybe she's changed too. But isn't that part of the journey? You're both here, in this moment, for a reason. Maybe it's worth exploring, even if it doesn't end the way you hope." Before he could reply, Smita caught his gaze from across the terrace, tilting her head slightly, as if to ask him to join her. He gave Shalini a grateful smile and made his way over to Smita, who was now leaning against the railing, gazing out at the ocean. The wind tugged at her hair, and she brushed it back absently, lost in thought. "Mind if I join you?" he asked, stopping beside her. "Not at all." She looked over, a faint smile playing on her lips. "It's nice to see you so… contemplative. I don't remember you being this serious in school." He chuckled, leaning against the railing beside her. "Life has a way of doing that, doesn't it? Turning us into versions of ourselves we never imagined we'd become."

She nodded, her gaze drifting back to the waves. "You're right. I guess we all carry things we didn't expect, burdens we didn't ask for." They stood in silence for a while, the sound of the ocean filling the space between them. He could feel the weight of her words, the unspoken pain that lingered beneath her calm exterior. "Smita," he began, his voice soft. "Do you ever wonder… what things might have been like if you hadn't left? If we'd had more time?" Her shoulders tensed slightly, and she didn't look at him right away. "Sometimes," she admitted, her voice barely above a whisper. "But I try not to dwell on it. Regret… it has a way of eating you up inside if you let it. And life goes on, whether we're ready for it or not." He watched her, feeling the urge to reach out, to offer her some comfort. But he sensed that she wasn't looking for consolation; she was searching for understanding. So, he simply nodded, respecting the boundaries she had built around herself.

"I don't regret meeting you, Smita," he said softly. "Or the time we had. And even though things didn't go the way I'd hoped, I'm grateful for it. You taught me more than you'll ever know." She looked at him then, her eyes softening, and for a moment, he saw a flicker of the girl he had fallen for all those years ago, the girl who had been his partner in crime, his confidante, his closest friend. "Thank you, Maverick," she whispered. "For saying that." They spent the rest of the evening talking, their conversation weaving between memories of their youth and the lives they had built since then. They laughed over old stories, filling in the gaps in each other's memories, and shared stories of the challenges and triumphs that had shaped them. With each word, he felt their connection deepen, as if they were slowly bridging the distance that had grown between them over the years.

But as the night wore on, Maverick noticed a shadow in her gaze, a sadness that seemed to grow with each passing hour. He wanted to ask her about it, to understand what burden she was carrying. But he knew that some things couldn't be forced, that she would share her secrets when she was ready. As they prepared to leave, Smita glanced at him, her expression hesitant. "Maverick, would you… would you like to meet again? Just the two of us?" He felt his heart quicken, a thrill running through him at the thought of spending more time with her. "I'd like that," he replied, unable to hide his smile. They exchanged numbers, and she promised to call him soon. As they said their goodbyes and went their separate ways, Maverick felt a surge of anticipation, a sense of hope that he hadn't felt in years.

The next day, Maverick found himself thinking about Smita constantly. He was in his office, attempting to focus on his work, but her face kept drifting into his thoughts, her words echoing in his mind. He thought of the sadness in her gaze, the vulnerability she had allowed him to see, and he felt an overwhelming urge to protect her, to be there for her in whatever way she needed. That evening, he received a message from her, a simple "Can we meet? Tomorrow evening?" He replied with a quick "Yes," his heart racing at the thought of seeing her again. The following evening, they met at a quiet café, tucked away in a hidden corner of the city. The place was cosy and intimate, with soft lighting and gentle music playing in the background. They found a secluded corner, and for a while, they simply talked, picking up where they had left off the night before.

But tonight, Maverick could sense a shift in Smita's demeanour. She seemed more reserved, as if something was weighing on her mind. "Smita, is everything okay?" he asked gently, his eyes searching her face. She took a deep breath, her hands clasped together on the table. "Maverick, there's something I need to tell you," she said quietly. "Something I should have told you a long time ago." He felt a pang of worry, a flicker of fear at the intensity in her gaze. But he nodded, bracing himself for whatever she was about to say. "There was… someone else," she said, her voice barely audible. "After I moved away. I met someone, and we… we fell in love. I thought he was my future, that he would be the person I'd spend my life with." She paused, her gaze fixed on her hands. "But things didn't go as planned. It ended… badly. And I was left with nothing but regret."

Maverick felt his heart sink, a mixture of emotions swirling within him. He hadn't expected this, hadn't imagined that she had loved someone else in the time they'd been apart. But he could see the pain in her eyes, the regret and sadness that had been lingering in the background of their conversations. "Smita, I… I'm sorry," he said softly. "I didn't know." She looked at him, her eyes filled with tears. "I didn't want you to know. I thought that if I could just move on, if I could leave it all behind, I might be able to find happiness again. But it's been so hard, Maverick. I don't know if I can ever feel that way again." He reached across the table, taking her hand in his. "You don't have to carry this alone, Smita. I'm here. And whatever happens, I'll be here for you." For the first time, he saw a glimmer of hope in her gaze, a spark that hadn't been there before. And in that moment, he knew that he would do whatever it took to help her heal, to show her that she could trust him, that she could find happiness again—even if it took a lifetime.

They stayed at the café long after it closed, talking about the past, the present, and the future they dared to imagine. And as they finally parted ways, Maverick felt a sense of peace, a certainty that no matter what lay ahead, he had found his way back to the person he had always loved.

CHAPTER 4

BRIDGING THE PAST AND PRESENT

A few days after their emotional café meeting, Maverick felt a tug in his chest every time he thought of Smita. As much as he longed for them to pick up where they left off, there was an undeniable awareness of the uncertainties between them, a gulf formed by years apart and lives lived on different paths. They met again one evening in a quiet part of the city, under the canopy of a serene park. The evening air was crisp, carrying the scent of blooming flowers, and the gentle hum of city life faded into the background. It was an unspoken agreement to meet in a place that would allow them to escape the distractions of the world for a while. As they strolled side by side, their conversations alternated between light-hearted reminisces and reflective silences. There was comfort in their shared memories but also a sense of fragility. Smita seemed more relaxed, yet her gaze would sometimes wander, a flicker of doubt clouding her eyes. Maverick noticed it, unsure whether to address it directly or to let her navigate her own pace.

Eventually, they stopped at a bench overlooking a small pond. Smita broke the silence first, her voice steady but filled with a sense of resolve. "Maverick, do you ever wonder if things would be easier if we'd never reconnected?" The question caught him off guard, and he glanced at her, seeing the seriousness in her expression. "Easier?" he echoed, thinking it over. "Maybe. But that doesn't mean it would be better. I don't want to spend the rest of my life wondering, 'What if.' Do you?" She shook her head, a soft sigh escaping her. "No. I don't want to live with regret. But sometimes, I feel like there's a part of me that's still holding back. After everything that's happened, there's a fear I can't shake—a fear of being hurt again." Maverick reached for her hand, giving it a gentle squeeze. "I understand, Smita. And I won't pretend that I can magically take that fear away. But I want you to know that I'm here, and I'm willing to work through this with you. We don't have to rush. We can take it one step at a time and see where this journey leads us."

She looked down at their intertwined hands, a small, grateful smile curving her lips. "I appreciate that, Maverick. More than you know." There was a softness in her voice that warmed him, a vulnerability she was finally allowing him to see. They sat in silence for a while, watching the gentle ripples on the pond. Eventually, Maverick spoke, his tone thoughtful. "You know, life has a funny way of circling back to things we think we've left behind. It brings people back into our lives when we least expect it. Maybe… maybe this is our second chance. A chance to build something from the pieces of what we once had." She turned to him, her eyes shining with a mixture of hope and hesitation. "Do you really believe that? That people can reconnect after so much time has passed and still build something meaningful?" "I do," he replied, his gaze steady. "I think that sometimes, distance can give us the perspective we need to understand ourselves and each other better. And I think it's worth the effort if we're both willing to try."

Smita smiled, though her expression was tinged with a trace of doubt. "It sounds so simple when you say it. But… what if it doesn't work out? What if, after all this, we end up hurting each other again?" Maverick thought for a moment, considering her words. "I can't promise that it'll be perfect, Smita. And I can't promise that we won't face challenges. But I believe that we owe it to ourselves to try. And if we're honest with each other, if we approach this with openness and understanding, maybe we can avoid the mistakes of the past." A silence fell between them, but it wasn't the uneasy silence of before. This was a silence of shared understanding, a recognition that they were both carrying the same hope and fear, and that they were both willing to take the risk, however uncertain the outcome might be.

Over the next few weeks, they began to see each other more frequently, gradually weaving themselves into each other's lives. They explored new places in the city, discovering cosy cafés, hidden bookstores, and art galleries. Each encounter added a new layer to their relationship, building a foundation that felt both familiar and refreshingly new. But even as they grew closer, they remained aware of the unspoken questions that lingered between them. Both were cautious, afraid of moving too quickly, yet each tentative step forward strengthened the bond they were rebuilding.

One evening, they found themselves at Smita's apartment, sharing a quiet dinner she had prepared. As they lingered over dessert, Maverick noticed a framed photograph on a nearby shelf, a picture of Smita with her family from years ago. The image stirred a curiosity he hadn't expressed before, and he hesitated before asking, "Tell me about them, about your life after you moved away. I want to know the parts of you I missed."

Smita paused, her expression thoughtful as she traced the rim of her glass with her finger. "It's strange, but talking about my past feels… difficult, almost as if it belongs to someone else. I became someone different after I left. Part of that was necessity—adapting to new places, new people. And part of it was… survival. I learned to guard my heart, to keep people at a distance." Maverick nodded, sensing the weight of her words. "That makes sense. Sometimes life forces us to put up walls, to protect ourselves from getting hurt." She looked at him, a flicker of vulnerability in her eyes. "But I don't want to keep those walls up with you. I'm learning to let them down, slowly… It's just, sometimes I wonder if you'll still want to know me once you see all of me—the parts that aren't as… beautiful." He reached across the table, taking her hand in his. "Smita, I'm not here for just the good parts. I want to know all of you, the real you. And whatever we find along the way, we'll face it together."

Her gaze softened, and she squeezed his hand, a grateful smile breaking through her hesitation. "Thank you, Maverick. For being patient with me." Their evenings together became a sanctuary, a space where they could be vulnerable and unguarded. Smita began sharing stories from her past, moments of heartbreak, struggles she had faced, dreams she had abandoned. And with each story, Maverick felt his admiration for her grow, realising the depth of resilience and courage she possessed. In turn, he opened up to her about his own struggles, the lonely nights, the missed opportunities, the times he had doubted his own path. They laughed together, cried together, and found solace in each other's stories, their shared vulnerability forging a bond that went beyond mere attraction.

But even as they grew closer, the future loomed like an uncharted horizon, filled with questions neither of them could answer. They were both aware of the possibility that this might not work out, that the past could resurface in ways they hadn't anticipated. Yet, despite the uncertainty, they were willing to take the risk, knowing that some things were worth fighting for. One evening, as they sat in Smita's living room, she turned to him, her expression serious yet hopeful. "Maverick, I think… I think I'm ready to take this leap with you to see where this journey takes us." He felt a surge of relief and joy, a warmth spreading through his chest. "I've been waiting for this moment, Smita. And whatever happens, we'll face it together." They embraced, holding each other close as the weight of their shared decision settled over them. It wasn't a promise of perfection but a promise of commitment, a pledge to navigate the complexities of their relationship with honesty and understanding.

In the days that followed, they faced both challenges and triumphs, moments of doubt and moments of pure joy. Their journey was anything but straightforward, but each step brought them closer, their love deepening with every experience they shared. And as they looked toward the future, they knew that whatever lay ahead, they had finally found something worth holding on to, something that had survived the trials of time and distance, a love that was both fragile and unbreakable, a love that would guide them through whatever challenges awaited.

CHAPTER 5

UNCHARTED PATHS

Months passed, and the connection between Maverick and Smita strengthened with each new chapter of their lives together. Their relationship had become a dance of discovery, one where they carefully navigated each other's emotions, histories, and aspirations. With every step forward, they grew more intertwined, even as they encountered the challenges of merging two lives that had once taken vastly different paths. The first major milestone came in the form of an invitation. Maverick was hosting a gallery show, a culmination of months of his work that explored themes of time, memory, and resilience. It was his first exhibit in years, and he felt both exhilarated and vulnerable, knowing that Smita would be there, seeing his soul laid bare through his art.

On the evening of the show, Smita arrived wearing a simple yet elegant dress, her excitement and pride evident in her eyes. She wove through the crowd until she found him, standing by one of his paintings, an abstract piece with bold strokes and muted colours that seemed to capture the essence of longing. "Maverick, this is incredible," she whispered as she reached him, her gaze filled with admiration. "I can feel every emotion you poured into these pieces. It's like each brushstroke tells a story." He smiled, his heart swelling with gratitude and pride. "Thank you, Smita. Having you here means more than you know." They stood together, their hands brushing as they took in the exhibit, sharing glances and silent affirmations as the evening unfolded.

But as the night progressed, Maverick couldn't help but notice a subtle shift in her demeanour. A few times, he caught her glancing away, her expression thoughtful and distant, as if something weighed on her mind. He didn't press her about it that night, choosing instead to savour the success of the show and her presence by his side. It wasn't until a few days later, during a quiet evening at her apartment, that he gently broached the topic. "I noticed you seemed a bit… distracted at the gallery," he began, his tone cautious yet curious. "Is everything okay?" Smita hesitated, her gaze fixed on a spot on the floor before meeting his eyes. "I loved your work, Maverick. And I'm so proud of you for putting it out there. It's just… sometimes, I wonder where I fit into all of this." She paused, her voice soft. "Your art, your ambitions, your world—it's all so vast and vibrant. And sometimes, I feel like I'm still trying to find my place in it."

He reached for her hand, his expression gentle. "Smita, you're already a part of my world. Your presence, your support, it means everything to me. But if you're feeling uncertain, let's talk about it. I don't want you to feel like you're on the outside." She looked at him, her eyes filled with a mixture of gratitude and vulnerability. "I guess it's just the old fears creeping in, the doubts that tell me I might not be enough for you, that maybe I can't keep up with the life you've built." Maverick pulled her closer, his voice soft but firm. "Smita, you are more than enough. And I'm not looking for someone to 'keep up' with me. I'm looking for someone to walk beside me and share this journey with. You don't have to prove anything to me—you just have to be yourself."

His words seemed to ease some of her uncertainty, and she leaned into him, allowing herself to believe in his reassurance. Yet, beneath her acceptance, there was a lingering hesitation, a silent question about whether she could truly find her place in his world without losing herself. As their relationship deepened, they began to discuss the future more openly, exploring the possibility of living together, building a life as partners. They talked about dreams and plans, weaving visions of a shared future that felt both thrilling and daunting. But with each new step, they faced the challenges that came with blending two lives shaped by different experiences. The first real test of their relationship came when Smita received an unexpected job offer, a position that would require her to relocate to another city, albeit temporarily. It was an opportunity she had always dreamed of, a chance to work on a project that aligned with her passion and ambitions. But it also meant putting distance between her and Maverick, just as they were beginning to build something meaningful.

When she broke the news to him, his initial reaction was a mixture of pride and concern. "This is an incredible opportunity, Smita. I'm so happy for you. But... have you thought about how this might impact us?" She nodded, her expression conflicted. "I have. And honestly, I don't want to lose what we have. But this is a chance I may not get again, and I feel like I need to take it. For me. For my own growth." Maverick took a deep breath, processing her words. "I understand, Smita. And I want you to follow your dreams, to pursue what makes you happy. I'll support you, no matter what. But… I'll miss you." She reached for his hand, her gaze filled with determination and warmth. "We can make this work, Maverick. I believe in us. I know it won't be easy, but if we're both committed, we can find a way to stay connected."

Their decision to embrace a long-distance relationship tested their commitment, pushing them to communicate more openly, to find new ways to maintain their connection. Late-night phone calls, shared photos, and video chats became their lifeline, bridging the physical distance with moments of closeness that kept them grounded in each other's lives. Over time, they learned to navigate the complexities of their situation, finding strength in their shared determination to make it work. But even as they grew more resilient, they couldn't ignore the challenges that came with being apart, the missed moments, the longing, the sense of incompleteness that lingered in their hearts. One evening, as they talked over the phone, Maverick shared a thought that had been on his mind for a while. "Smita, I don't want us to live like this forever. I want to build a life with you, a life where we don't have to say goodbye at the end of every call."

She was silent for a moment, her voice soft when she finally responded. "I want that too, Maverick. More than anything. But I don't want to rush into something we're not ready for. Let's take it one step at a time, see where this journey takes us. I believe that if we're meant to be together, we'll find a way." Their conversations about the future became more frequent, filled with dreams of a life where they could wake up beside each other, share quiet mornings and late-night talks. And while they both acknowledged the uncertainties that lay ahead, their commitment to each other remained steadfast, a beacon of hope that guided them through the challenges of distance. As the months passed, they found a rhythm that worked for them, a balance between their individual pursuits and their shared dreams. Their love grew stronger, tempered by the trials they had endured, and they began to see the possibility of a future that was both grounded in reality and brimming with promise.

And so, they continued to build their life together, one step at a time, knowing that the path ahead would be filled with both challenges and joys. They embraced the uncertainty with open hearts, choosing to believe in the power of their love to overcome whatever obstacles lay in their way. In the quiet moments, as they held each other close, they knew that their journey was far from over, that there would be new milestones to reach, new challenges to face. But for now, they were content, grateful for the chance to build something beautiful from the fragments of their past—a love that had endured, a love that had grown stronger with each passing day.

CHAPTER 6

TRIALS OF TIME

As Maverick and Smita's long-distance relationship continued, their commitment to one another deepened, but so did the realities and challenges of their situation. They had woven together a fragile balance, relying on communication, trust, and shared dreams to keep their love alive. Yet, both knew that life had its way of testing even the strongest bonds, and soon enough, their resilience would be put to the ultimate test. One evening, after another week of long phone calls and shared messages, Maverick sat by his studio window, watching the city lights flicker against the night sky. A part of him yearned for Smita's presence, for the warmth of her laughter filling his home, and the simple comfort of her hand in his. The distance, once manageable, was beginning to weigh on him, its presence like a shadow that grew longer each day.

During one of their video calls, Maverick broached a subject that had been on his mind. "Smita," he began, his tone measured but laced with a hint of anxiety, "do you ever think about… what comes next? I mean, with us, with this distance?" Smita hesitated, her gaze dropping before she looked back at him. "I do, Maverick. More often than you might realise. I want to be with you, to share a life with you without having to count the days until our next call." She paused, a look of vulnerability crossing her face. "But I also have commitments here, projects I need to see through. And I worry that if I come back too soon, I'll be giving up a part of myself."

Maverick nodded, understanding yet struggling with his own longing. "I know, Smita. And I don't want you to compromise who you are or what you're passionate about. But I can't deny that this distance… it's hard." His voice softened, and he looked at her, his eyes filled with both love and a touch of sadness. "I just want to know if there's a way for us to bridge this gap, to find a path forward that honours both of us." The conversation hung between them, heavy and unresolved, as they struggled to find answers that seemed elusive. In the days that followed, they carried on as they always had, trying to push away the questions that lingered in the back of their minds. But with each passing day, the weight of their unspoken worries grew, casting a shadow over even their happiest moments.

Their next challenge came when Smita's work became increasingly demanding, leaving her with little time to connect with Maverick. She often returned home exhausted, barely able to muster the energy for a short conversation before falling asleep. For Maverick, the distance felt wider than ever, a gulf that no amount of phone calls could bridge. He found himself wondering if this was the beginning of the end, if they were slowly drifting apart despite their love. One night, after days of strained interactions, Maverick decided to visit Smita without telling her. He wanted to surprise her, to rekindle the spark that had once burned so brightly between them. Arriving in her city, he booked a room at a nearby hotel and made his way to her apartment, his heart pounding with anticipation. But when he knocked on her door, he was met with an unexpected sight.

Smita opened the door, surprised and visibly caught off guard. She was dressed casually, her hair tousled from a long day, but Maverick could sense a subtle tension in her demeanour. She welcomed him inside, though her smile seemed hesitant, as if she were struggling to bridge the emotional distance that had grown between them. As they sat down, Maverick reached for her hand, his expression earnest. "I missed you, Smita. I couldn't stand being apart any longer. I wanted to surprise you, to remind you how much I care." She smiled, though there was a flicker of something else in her eyes—a mixture of exhaustion and uncertainty. "I missed you too, Maverick. But... things have been so overwhelming lately. I barely have time for myself, let alone for us." She took a deep breath, her voice faltering. "I don't want to lose what we have, but sometimes I wonder if this distance is taking more from us than it's giving."

His heart sank, but he forced himself to remain composed. "Smita, I get it. I know you're working hard, and I don't want to add to your stress. But I'm here because I believe in us, because I think we can make this work. If we both want it enough." Smita looked at him, her gaze filled with conflicting emotions. "I do want us to work, Maverick. I just... I don't know if we can keep doing this, always compromising, always trying to make time. I wonder if we're both holding on to something that might not be sustainable." The words struck Maverick like a blow, and for a moment, he struggled to respond. He looked into her eyes, searching for a sign that this was just a passing doubt, that her love for him was still as strong as his for her. But all he saw was the uncertainty that mirrored his own fears, the questions that had lingered between them for too long.

"Are you saying you want to end this?" he asked, his voice barely above a whisper. She shook her head, her expression pained. "No, Maverick. I'm saying I don't know what the future holds for us. I don't want to give up on what we have, but I don't want to keep hurting each other by trying to force something that might not be meant to last." They sat in silence, each lost in their thoughts, the weight of their situation pressing down on them. For the first time, they faced the possibility that love might not be enough to bridge the gap between their dreams and realities. It was a sobering realisation, one that left them both questioning the path they had chosen. In the days that followed, they took time apart to reflect, giving each other the space to search their hearts for answers. They knew that whatever decision they made would have lasting consequences, that the future of their relationship depended on their ability to confront their fears and find a way forward that honoured both their love and their individuality.

When they finally came together to talk, there was a newfound clarity in their eyes, a sense of acceptance that hadn't been there before. They spoke openly about their needs, their dreams, and their fears, acknowledging the pain of their situation and the love that had brought them together. And at that moment, they made a choice—not to force a future that might be unsustainable, but to trust in the journey they had shared, to honour the love that had brought them together even if it meant letting go. It was a bittersweet decision, one that left them with both a sense of loss and a profound gratitude for the time they had spent together. They parted with a promise to remain in each other's lives, to carry the memory of their love as a source of strength and inspiration. And though their paths would lead them in different directions, they knew that they would always hold a special place in each other's hearts, a bond that transcended time and distance.

As Maverick walked away, he felt a mixture of sorrow and peace, a quiet understanding that their love had been a gift, a chapter in his life that he would carry with him, no matter where the future might lead. And though the road ahead was uncertain, he knew that he had been forever changed by the love they had shared, a love that would remain a part of him, always.

THE ECHOES OF US

Months passed, each one a mixture of change and quiet transformation as Maverick and Smita embarked on separate journeys of growth and healing. Their parting, though painful, had marked the beginning of a new chapter for each of them, a chance to rediscover themselves and honour the love they had shared in a way that would always remain with them, just beyond the reach of everyday life. For Maverick, the quiet solitude of his days allowed him to focus more deeply on his art. His studio became a sanctuary where he poured his emotions onto the canvas, capturing fragments of memories and moments from his time with Smita. He found himself painting scenes that were both vibrant and haunting, images that mirrored the beauty and ache of his memories with her. He realised that, through their relationship, he had discovered a new layer of himself—an emotional depth that now bled into every piece he created.

One painting in particular captured his heart, an image of two figures walking along a beach at dusk, hands nearly touching but separated by the delicate pull of the ocean tide. He titled it "The Echoes of Us," a tribute to the love they had shared, a love that had become an indelible part of him. He exhibited this painting at a local gallery, and it quickly became a favourite among visitors. People were drawn to its raw vulnerability, sensing the story behind it even if they didn't know its details. Watching others connect with the work, Maverick felt a quiet pride, knowing that he had transformed his love and loss into something beautiful and lasting.

Meanwhile, Smita embraced her work with renewed purpose. Though she missed Maverick deeply, she recognised that their time together had gifted her with a sense of courage and openness she had previously lacked. Their love had taught her to face her fears, to open her heart, and to trust in herself. She threw herself into her projects, using her work to advocate for causes close to her heart, her passion echoing the kindness and empathy she had shared with Maverick. She travelled to new cities, speaking to crowds and working with communities, each experience a step forward in her journey of self-discovery. And as she moved through her days, she carried with her a quiet strength, a resilience that came from knowing she had loved deeply and been loved in return.

One evening, while returning from a conference, Smita received an email with a photo attached. It was from Maverick—a simple snapshot of his painting, **The Echoes of Us**, now hanging in a prominent spot in the gallery. He wrote a brief note:

"I wanted you to see this. This painting was inspired by us, by everything we shared. I hope it brings you the same peace it brought me."

As she looked at the image, a sense of bittersweet joy filled her heart. She knew that their love had been far from perfect, but it had been real, and it had changed her in ways she would carry for a lifetime. Their journey had ended, but its impact lingered like an echo, a reminder that sometimes the most profound connections are those that leave us with lessons that shape who we are. Years passed, and though they each moved on, Maverick and Smita never forgot the bond they had shared. They continued to exchange occasional notes and updates, small glimpses into each other's lives that reminded them of the journey they had once embarked on together.

One day, Maverick received a message from Smita with a simple line: **"Thank you for being a part of my story."**

He replied, his heart warmed by the quiet grace of her words. **"And thank you for being a part of mine. Our story will always be a cherished chapter."**

And so, though their paths would remain separate, they knew they had left an indelible mark on each other's lives, a love that had transformed, endured, and evolved into a lasting, intangible presence. It was a testament to the beauty of human connection, a reminder that love, in all its forms, can be both fleeting and forever.

As they continued forward, carrying their memories like cherished keepsakes, they understood that their story would live on, not in physical closeness or shared daily moments, but in the quiet resonance of two souls who had once walked hand in hand, leaving footprints on each other's hearts.

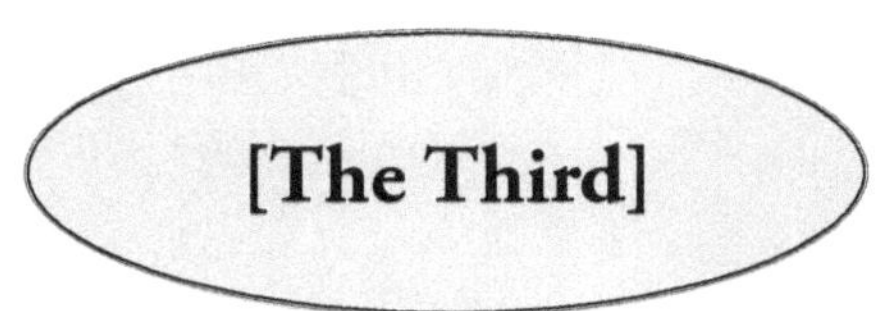

[The Third]

Echoes of Veiled Desires

I

It was the dawn of a new era in Delhi, the early 2000s – a time when India's capital was burgeoning with growth and ambition. The city's skyline, once dominated by ancient monuments and colonial relics, was now being dotted with modern high-rises, gleaming with glass and steel. At the heart of this transformation was Connaught Place, a historic district now housing some of the country's most influential corporate offices. One such office belonged to TechConnect Solutions, a leading IT company riding the wave of the tech boom. The office, occupying several floors of a newly constructed tower, buzzed with the energy of young professionals eager to leave their mark on the rapidly expanding digital landscape. The open-plan design fostered collaboration but also allowed for the careful observation of everyone's movements – a place where innovation thrived, but so did the rumours.

Among the many faces in this sea of ambition were Lawrence D'Souza and Advika Mehta. A recent transplant from Bangalore, Lawrence, had joined the company as a mid-level manager in the marketing department. At thirty-two, he was already making waves with his sharp analytical skills and strategic thinking. His rise in the industry had been swift, a result of his relentless drive and focus. But the move to Delhi had been as much a personal decision as a professional one. After a painful breakup with his long time girlfriend, Lawrence had needed a change – a fresh start in a city where no one knew his story. Despite his outward confidence, Lawrence was still grappling with the loneliness that came from leaving behind his familiar life.

Advika was a senior software developer who had been with TechConnect Solutions for five years. At twenty-nine, she was one of the company's most valuable assets, her technical skills earning her the respect of her peers and superiors alike. But Advika was not just known for her proficiency with code; she was also admired for her composure under pressure. She kept to herself, avoiding the office's social cliques and steering clear of the gossip mill. Her reserved nature was partly due to her upbringing in a conservative Delhi family, where reputation and propriety were paramount. Advika had always been careful to separate her personal life from her professional one, knowing that any misstep could bring unwelcome scrutiny from both her family and her colleagues.

The first time Lawrence and Advika truly noticed each other was in a meeting that should have been routine but quickly became anything but. The company was about to embark on a major project – a high-stake pitch to secure a lucrative contract with a multinational client. The project team was carefully selected, and both Lawrence and Advika were among those chosen. The meeting room was filled with the usual suspects – department heads, key managers, and a few select staff members. As they discussed strategies and deadlines, Lawrence found himself intrigued by Advika's quiet but firm contributions. She didn't speak often, but when she did, her words carried weight. Lawrence, who was used to leading discussions, was impressed by how effortlessly she commanded respect with her knowledge.

Advika, on the other hand, noticed Lawrence's sharp mind and how he could quickly assess a situation and propose a solution. He was confident but not overbearing, a rare quality in the corporate world. She had heard of his reputation – how he had been brought in to shake things up in the marketing department – and she could see why he was considered an asset. As the meeting wrapped up, their eyes met briefly across the table. It was just a moment, a fleeting connection, but it left both of them feeling something unexpected – a spark of curiosity, perhaps, or the first hint of an attraction that neither of them was willing to acknowledge just yet.

II

The corporate culture at TechConnect Solutions was a blend of high pressure and high reward. The office was a microcosm of the broader city – fast-paced, competitive, and unforgiving to those who faltered. Promotions were earned through hard work, but just as often through strategic alliances and careful navigation of office politics. Everyone knew that success here required not just skill but also the ability to play the game.

Lawrence, with his recent arrival, was still learning the unwritten rules. His team was composed of bright, ambitious individuals, many of whom were eager to impress the new manager. He quickly established himself as a leader who valued results, but also someone who encouraged his team to think creatively. This approach won him both admirers and rivals. Advika, on the other hand, had long mastered the art of surviving in this environment. Her reputation for excellence in her work meant she rarely had to involve herself in the petty rivalries that consumed others. But her aloofness also made her somewhat of an enigma. Colleagues respected her, but few truly knew her. She maintained a careful distance, aware that any misstep could impact her career and her standing within her family.

The project Lawrence and Advika were working on – a critical client pitch for a large international telecommunications company – demanded long hours and intense collaboration. As the project progressed, their professional admiration for each other deepened. They spent countless hours in the office, sometimes late into the night, poring over strategies, refining presentations, and troubleshooting issues. It was during these late-night sessions that their interactions became more personal. In the quiet of the nearly empty office, away from the eyes of their colleagues, they found themselves sharing more than just work-related discussions. Lawrence, who had always been a private person, began to open up to Advika about his struggles with adapting to life in Delhi. He spoke of the cultural differences he was still getting used to, and the loneliness that often crept in during his off-hours.

Advika, in turn, shared glimpses of her life outside of work – her close-knit but traditional family, the pressure to conform to societal expectations, and the challenge of balancing her professional ambitions with her personal responsibilities. She spoke of her parents' desire for her to settle down, and how they often reminded her that time was running out for her to find a suitable match. Despite her success at work, Advika carried the weight of her family's expectations, which sometimes felt suffocating. Their conversations, while still largely professional, began to touch on more personal topics. There was an unspoken understanding between them, a muted recognition of each other's struggles.

It was during one of these conversations that Lawrence found himself noticing details about Advika that he hadn't before – the way she brushed a stray strand of hair behind her ear, the faint dimple that appeared when she smiled, the intensity in her eyes when she spoke passionately about her work. Advika, too, began to see Lawrence in a different light. He was not just the confident, ambitious manager she had first met. There was a vulnerability to him, a depth that she found increasingly intriguing. She admired his resilience, his ability to adapt, and the quiet strength he displayed in the face of challenges.

As their connection grew, so did the complexity of their feelings. Lawrence's background as a Catholic from Bangalore had always set him slightly apart in the largely Hindu-dominated environment of Delhi. His upbringing had been liberal but deeply rooted in the traditions of his faith. Moving to Delhi had been a professional decision, but it also represented a break from the life he had known. His family, though supportive of his career, had expressed concern about him living so far from home, especially after his breakup. Lawrence, however, saw this move as an opportunity to redefine himself, even if it meant facing the challenges of being an outsider in a city that often felt overwhelming.

Advika's life, on the other hand, was steeped in the traditions and expectations of her conservative Delhi family. As the eldest daughter, much was expected of her – both professionally and personally. Her family took great pride in her accomplishments at work, but they also reminded her constantly that her success would mean little if she did not eventually marry and start a family of her own. Advika had always been the dutiful daughter, balancing her career with the expectations placed on her. But as she grew closer to Lawrence, she found herself questioning the path that had been laid out for her.

The attraction between them, though still unspoken, became increasingly difficult to ignore. It was in the small moments that the tension between them was most palpable – a lingering glance during a meeting, the brief touch of hands as they passed documents back and forth, the way their conversations would sometimes veer into more personal territory before they quickly steered them back to work. One evening, after an especially long day, they found themselves alone in the office. The rest of the team had left, and the city outside was quiet; the usual bustle of Connaught Place was reduced to the distant hum of traffic. As they sat side by side, going over the final details of the pitch, the conversation once again drifted away from work.

They spoke about the challenges they faced in their respective roles, the pressures they felt, and the uncertainties about the future. Lawrence, feeling the weight of the day, admitted that he sometimes wondered if he had made the right choice moving to Delhi. Advika, in a rare moment of vulnerability, confessed that she often felt trapped between her family's expectations and her own aspirations. There was a silence between them after that, one filled with unspoken words and growing tension. Lawrence looked at Advika, noticing how the soft glow of the desk lamp highlighted her features, making her appear even more beautiful than he remembered.

He felt a sudden, overwhelming urge to reach out to her, to bridge the gap that had slowly been closing between them. Advika, sensing the shift in the atmosphere, felt her heart race. She could see the conflict in Lawrence's eyes, a mirror of the turmoil she felt within herself. But just as quickly as the moment had arrived, it passed. Lawrence, ever the professional, cleared his throat and suggested they call it a night. Advika agreed, grateful for the reprieve, but also unable to shake the feeling that something significant had just transpired between them. As they gathered their things and left the office, both Lawrence and Advika knew that what had started as a simple professional relationship was becoming something far more complicated.

III

As the days turned into weeks, the connection between Lawrence and Advika deepened. Their interactions, initially driven by professional necessity, became more personal with each passing day. They began to seek each other out, not just for work-related matters, but for the comfort and understanding that only the other seemed able to provide. Their conversations expanded beyond the confines of the office. They would often grab a quick lunch together at a nearby café or take short breaks on the rooftop terrace, where they could talk without the fear of prying eyes.

The intensity of their bond was undeniable, yet both were acutely aware of the precarious nature of their growing relationship. In a workplace where professional boundaries were strictly maintained, and office romances were frowned upon, their connection was a ticking time bomb. The unspoken rules of corporate life loomed over them, reminding them that what they were feeling could lead to disastrous consequences if it ever came to light.

The more time they spent together, the more Lawrence and Advika found themselves struggling with the ethical implications of their relationship. They both knew that a romance between them could jeopardise not only their jobs but also their reputations within the company. For Lawrence, the dilemma was particularly acute. He was still relatively new to the company and to Delhi, and any misstep could derail his career. He had worked hard to earn the respect of his colleagues, and he was determined to continue his upward trajectory. But with every passing day, it became harder to ignore the feelings he had for Advika. He found himself constantly distracted, his thoughts drifting to her during meetings, his heart racing whenever they were alone together.

Advika faced a different but equally challenging ethical dilemma. Her position in the company was secure, but she knew that a scandal could undo years of hard work. She had built her reputation on professionalism and competence, and she was painfully aware that a relationship with Lawrence could tarnish that image. Moreover, she feared the potential fallout within her family. They had always trusted her judgement, but she knew that they would disapprove of a workplace romance, especially one with someone outside their community. As they continued to work closely together, the tension between their professional responsibilities and personal desires grew. Both were torn between the fear of losing everything they had worked for and the irresistible pull they felt toward each other.

The cultural and social pressures that weighed on Advika were significant. Raised in a conservative Hindu family in Delhi, she was constantly reminded of the importance of maintaining her family's honour and adhering to societal expectations. Her parents, though proud of her professional achievements, frequently hinted at the need for her to settle down and marry. They had begun introducing her to potential suitors, men from similar backgrounds, with stable jobs and good family reputations. Advika, however, found herself increasingly disinterested in these meetings. Her thoughts were often elsewhere, with a man who, by all societal standards, was entirely unsuitable.

Lawrence, too, faced his own set of pressures. Although his family was more liberal, they had always emphasised the importance of stability and making prudent choices. His decision to move to Delhi had already been a bold step, and a relationship with a colleague, especially one fraught with potential complications, was not something they would support. Lawrence was also conscious of the cultural differences between him and Advika. Although they shared many values, he knew that their backgrounds were worlds apart. He often wondered if they were setting themselves up for failure by pursuing something that might never work in the long run. These cultural and social pressures only added to the complexity of their situation. While their bond grew stronger with each passing day, the external forces pulling them apart became more formidable.

The tension between them reached a new height during a team outing. The company had organised a weekend retreat at a resort on the outskirts of Delhi, ostensibly for team building but also as a reward for the hard work everyone had put into the recent project. The atmosphere was relaxed, and the usual formality of the office was replaced by casual conversations and light-hearted banter. Lawrence and

Advika tried to maintain a professional distance, aware that their colleagues were always watching. But as the day wore on and the team settled into the evening with drinks and laughter, the lines between professional and personal began to blur.

After dinner, the group gathered around a bonfire, where stories and jokes were shared. Lawrence and Advika found themselves sitting next to each other, the warmth of the fire doing little to ease the tension between them. As the night progressed and their colleagues began to retire to their rooms, Lawrence and Advika lingered, caught in the glow of the flames and the quiet of the night. They talked softly, their conversation gradually shifting from the safe topics of work to more personal matters. The night felt like a bubble, isolated from the reality of their daily lives. For a moment, it was just the two of them, free from the constraints that had kept them apart.

But as they sat there, lost in each other's company, they didn't notice that one of their colleagues, Rajiv, had returned to the bonfire to retrieve his forgotten phone. He saw them, their heads close together, and though he couldn't hear what they were saying, the intimacy of their posture spoke volumes. Rajiv didn't say anything, but his lingering glances as he left sent a shiver down Advika's spine. She knew that rumours could start from the smallest of incidents, and their situation was already precarious enough without the added scrutiny. Lawrence, sensing her discomfort, suggested they call it a night. They walked back to their rooms in silence, the weight of what had almost happened hanging between them.

The following Monday, the office buzzed with post-retreat chatter. As Lawrence and Advika entered the building, they couldn't help but feel a sense of unease. Both were on edge, wondering if Rajiv had said anything or if their secret was still safe. They tried to act as if everything was normal, but the uncertainty gnawed at them. Throughout the day, they noticed subtle changes in their colleagues' behaviour - sideways glances, hushed conversations that stopped when they entered a room, and a general sense of tension that hadn't been there before. It was clear that something was amiss, but they couldn't be sure if it was related to them or if they were simply being paranoid.

Their work continued as usual, but the carefree nature of their interactions had vanished. Every conversation felt loaded, every meeting an exercise in restraint. The once easy camaraderie between them had been replaced by a strained formality that was almost unbearable. Lawrence and Advika knew that they were walking a fine line. The consequences of being discovered could be severe – both professionally and personally. Yet, despite the risks, the pull between them was stronger than ever. Each day they spent apart only heightened the tension, making it increasingly difficult to resist the attraction that had taken hold of them.

Their secret had become a burden, but it was one they couldn't seem to let go of. They were caught in a web of desire, duty, and fear, unsure of how to extricate themselves without losing everything in the process.

IV

The day of the crucial client pitch arrived with all the intensity and pressure that had been building up for weeks. The entire team at TechConnect Solutions was on edge, knowing that the outcome of this presentation could have significant implications for the company's future. Winning this contract with the international telecommunications giant would solidify its position in the market, while failure could spell disaster.

Lawrence and Advika, who had been at the heart of the project, felt the weight of responsibility more than anyone else. They had poured countless hours into preparing for this moment, fine-tuning every detail, rehearsing every possible scenario. Despite the tension that had grown between them in recent days, they managed to put their personal feelings aside, focusing entirely on the task at hand. The pitch took place in the company's sleek boardroom, with the client's executive joining via video conference from London. The presentation went smoothly, with Lawrence leading the discussion and Advika handling the technical aspects with her usual precision.

Their professional synergy was on full display, each complementing the other's strengths. As they fielded questions and addressed concerns, it was clear that their hard work had paid off. The clients were impressed, nodding in approval as the presentation wrapped up. When the meeting ended, there was a palpable sense of relief in the room. Their colleagues congratulated them with handshakes and pats on the back, acknowledging the successful pitch. Lawrence and Advika exchanged a glance – one that was meant to be celebratory, but instead was filled with unspoken emotion. It was a look that said everything they had been trying to avoid: the acknowledgement of what was simmering just beneath the surface.

The exhilaration of the successful pitch didn't last long for Lawrence and Advika. The adrenaline that had carried them through the presentation was quickly replaced by the unresolved tension that had been building for weeks. Both knew that they could no longer ignore what was happening between them. Later that evening, after most of the office had emptied out, Lawrence found Advika still working at her desk, reviewing the project's final details. The quiet of the office, combined with the dimming light outside, created an atmosphere of intimacy that neither of them could resist.

Lawrence hesitated for a moment, then walked over to her desk. "Advika," he said softly, his voice tinged with something more than just the usual professional tone. She looked up, her eyes meeting his, and for a moment, they simply stood there, the air between them thick with unspoken words. "I think we need to talk," Lawrence finally said, breaking the silence. Advika nodded, knowing exactly what he meant. "Not here," she replied, her voice barely above a whisper. They left the office together, stepping out into the cool night air. The streets of Connaught Place were still bustling, but they felt isolated, as if the world around them had faded into the background.

They walked in silence for a few minutes, each lost in their thoughts, until they reached a small park nearby. Finding a quiet bench, they sat down, the noise of the city distant enough to feel like a different world. Lawrence was the first to speak. "Advika, I can't stop thinking about you. About us." His words hung in the air, heavy with the weight of all they had been avoiding. Advika looked down at her hands, which were clenched in her lap. She had known this moment was coming, but now that it was here, she didn't know what to say. "I've been thinking about it too," she admitted. "But Lawrence, this… whatever this is… it's impossible. You know that."

"Maybe," Lawrence replied, his voice laced with frustration. "But I can't help how I feel. I've tried to push it aside, to focus on work, but it's there, Advika. Every time I see you, it's there." Advika closed her eyes, fighting back the emotions that threatened to overwhelm her. "I feel the same way," she said quietly. "But we have to be realistic. If anyone finds out about us… it could ruin everything. Our jobs, our reputations. I can't risk that. And I know you can't either." Lawrence ran a hand through his hair, exhaling deeply. "I know. But what do we do? Pretend this never happened? Go back to how things were before?"

"Can we?" Advika asked, her voice trembling slightly. "Can we just ignore it?" For a moment, neither of them spoke, the reality of their situation pressing down on them. They both knew that ignoring their feelings was easier said than done. The attraction between them was too strong, too undeniable to simply wish away. "I don't know," Lawrence finally admitted. "But I do know that I don't want to lose you. Not like this." Advika's heart ached at his words. She felt the same, but the fear of what they could lose was overpowering. "Lawrence, I don't want to lose you either. But maybe the best way to protect what we have is to keep things as they are. To not cross the line." "But we already have," Lawrence countered, his voice filled with the pain of that truth. "We crossed it the moment we started caring about each other more than just colleagues." Advika didn't respond, tears welling up in her eyes. She knew he was right, but the thought of what they were risking was too much for her to bear.

Their emotional conversation was interrupted by the shrill ring of Lawrence's phone. He frowned as he saw the caller ID – it was Rajiv, the colleague who had seen them at the bonfire during the retreat. Lawrence answered, his tone immediately cautious. "Rajiv, what's up?" he asked, trying to keep his voice steady. "Lawrence," Rajiv's voice came through the line, sounding far too casual. "Just thought I'd give you a heads-up. I've been hearing some interesting things around the office. It seems like people are starting to notice how much time you and Advika spend together." Lawrence's heart skipped a beat. He exchanged a glance with Advika, who had gone pale. "What are you talking about?" Lawrence asked, trying to keep his voice even.

"Come on, Lawrence," Rajiv continued, his tone dripping with insinuation. "I'm not the only one who saw you two getting cosy at the retreat. Word spreads fast in this place, you know that." Lawrence felt a wave of panic rising within him. "Rajiv, whatever you think you saw –" "Relax, I'm not going to say anything," Rajiv interrupted. "But let's just say I'm in a position where I could use a little support. There's a promotion coming up that I'm very interested in, and I'd hate for any rumours to get in the way of that." Lawrence's blood ran cold. The implication was clear – Rajiv was blackmailing him. If Lawrence didn't back him for the promotion, Rajiv would spread rumours that could destroy both Lawrence and Advika's careers.

"Are you threatening me, Rajiv?" Lawrence asked, his voice low and dangerous. "Of course not," Rajiv replied smoothly. "Just making a suggestion. You help me, I help you. It's a win-win." Lawrence was silent for a long moment, his mind racing. Rajiv was unscrupulous, the kind of person who would have no qualms about ruining someone else's career if it benefitted him. Lawrence knew that if Rajiv spread rumours about him and Advika, their reputations would be irreparably damaged, and their careers could be over.

"I'll think about it," Lawrence finally said, his voice tight. "Good. I knew you'd see reason," Rajiv replied, sounding pleased with himself. "Talk soon, Lawrence." As he hung up the phone, Lawrence turned to Advika, his face ashen. "Rajiv knows. And he's threatening to expose us unless I help him get a promotion." Advika stared at him in shock, her mind struggling to process the gravity of the situation. "What are we going to do?" she asked, her voice barely above a whisper. "I don't know," Lawrence admitted, feeling a sense of hopelessness was over him. "But we can't let him control us. We need to figure out a way to deal with this without letting it destroy everything we've worked for."

The next few days were a blur of anxiety and tension. Lawrence and Advika avoided each other at work, knowing that any interaction between them could be misconstrued and used against them. They were both on edge, constantly looking over their shoulders, fearing that Rajiv would make good on his threat. Finally, Advika decided that they needed to confront the issue head-on. She suggested they meet outside of work to discuss their options. Lawrence agreed, and they decided to meet at a quiet café far from the office, where they could talk without fear of being overheard. When they sat down across from each other, the weight of the situation hung heavily between them.

Lawrence looked exhausted; his usual confident demeanour replaced by a weariness that came from the constant stress of their predicament. Advika, too, looked strained, her usually calm exterior showing signs of cracks. "Lawrence, we can't go on like this," Advika said, her voice trembling. "Rajiv has us backed into a corner. If we give in to his demands, we're just as bad as he is. But if we don't, he'll ruin us." Lawrence nodded, his jaw clenched. "I know. But what choice do we have? If he spreads those rumours, it won't just be our jobs at risk. It'll be our reputations, our careers, everything we've worked for."

"I can't believe it's come to this," Advika said, shaking her head. "We were just trying to do our jobs. We didn't ask for any of this." "I know," Lawrence said softly. "But we need to decide how to move forward. We could go to HR, but that's risky. Rajiv could deny everything, and it would be our word against his." "And even if HR believes us, the damage could already be done," Advika added. "Once rumours start, it's hard to stop them." They sat in silence for a moment, each lost in their thoughts. Advika could feel the walls closing in around them, the pressure mounting with every passing second. She had always prided herself on her ability to handle difficult situations, but this felt like too much.

"Maybe we should just end it," Lawrence said suddenly, his voice heavy with resignation. "End what?" Advika asked, though she already knew what he meant. "Us. Whatever this is," Lawrence replied, his eyes filled with pain. "If we end it now, we can at least say that we didn't let it get out of hand. We can go back to being colleagues, nothing more. Maybe then, Rajiv will back off." Advika felt her heart break at his words. She knew he was right, but the thought of losing him – of going back to a time when they were just colleagues – was unbearable. She had grown to care for him deeply, more than she had ever intended. But now, it seemed like the only way to protect themselves.

"Maybe you're right," she said, her voice barely audible. "Maybe this is the only way." Lawrence reached across the table, taking her hand in his. "Advika, I don't want to lose you. But I don't see another way out." Advika squeezed his hand, fighting back tears. "I don't want to lose you either. But if ending this is the only way to protect ourselves, then…. maybe we have to." They sat there, holding hands, knowing that they were about to make a decision that would change everything.

As they grappled with their decision, the conversation turned to the deeper issues that had been simmering beneath the surface – the cultural differences between them, the expectations of their families, and the societal pressures that had brought them to this breaking point. "Lawrence, I know this isn't just about Rajiv," Advika said, her voice tinged with sadness. "It's about us and the reality that we come from two very different worlds. My family would never accept this. They would never accept you." Lawrence felt a pang of hurt at her words, though he knew they were true. "And my family would worry about how we could make this work, with all the differences between us," he admitted. "But I was willing to try; I still am."

"I don't doubt that," Advika said softly. "But sometimes, love isn't enough. Sometimes, the world around us is too strong, and we can't fight it." "Maybe you're right," Lawrence said, his voice heavy with resignation. "But it doesn't make it any easier to accept." They both knew that their cultural backgrounds had always been a factor, an undercurrent, which had influenced their relationship from the beginning. But now, as they faced the reality of their situation, those differences seemed insurmountable.

"I wish things were different," Advika said, her voice filled with regret. "I wish we didn't have to make this choice." "So do I," Lawrence replied. "But maybe this is for the best. Maybe it's better to end it now before we get in too deep." With those words, they both knew that the decision had been made. They would end their relationship, not because they didn't care for each other, but because they cared too much to risk everything they had worked for.

The decision to end their relationship was the hardest either of them had ever made. They returned to work the next day with heavy hearts, determined to put their feelings aside and focus on their careers. But the emotional toll was immense, and the strain of pretending that nothing had changed was almost unbearable. Lawrence and Advika threw themselves into their work, using it as a distraction from the pain of their decision.

But no matter how hard they tried, the connection between them was impossible to ignore. Every glance, every accidental touch, every shared memory only served to remind them of what they had lost. Despite their best efforts, the distance they tried to create between them only seemed to heighten the tension. Their colleagues noticed the change in their behaviour, the strained interactions, the lack of the usual camaraderie. But no one dared to ask questions, aware that something had shifted but unsure of what it was.

As the days turned into weeks, the pain of their separation began to fade, replaced by a dull ache that settled deep within them. They both knew that they had made the right choice, but that knowledge did little to ease the emptiness they felt. In the end, Lawrence and Advika had made the hard choice to protect their careers, their reputations, and their families. But in doing so, they had also sacrificed something far more precious – the chance at a love that, despite all the challenges, had the potential to be something truly extraordinary.

V

The days following their decision were marked by a heavy silence that seemed to echo in every corner of the office. Lawrence and Advika, once so closely connected, now operated on parallel tracks that rarely intersected. The dynamic between them had shifted; the easy camaraderie they once shared had been replaced by a distant formality. They were polite, professional, and distant – exactly what they needed to be, but nothing like what they wanted. Their colleagues, ever perceptive, sensed the change but couldn't quite place its cause. The rumours that Rajiv had hinted at never materialised into anything concrete, thanks in part to Lawrence's skillful manoeuvring and Advika's unwavering professionalism. But the tension between them was undeniable, and those closest to them couldn't help but notice that something was off.

Lawrence buried himself in his work, throwing all his energy into the projects at hand. The success of the recent client pitch had put him in the spotlight, and his supervisors were quick to reward him with more responsibilities and higher stakes. He was on the fast track to a promotion, exactly where he had always wanted to be. Yet, the satisfaction he expected to feel was absent. The thrill of success was dulled by the loss he carried with him, a loss that no amount of professional achievement could fill.

Advika, too, focused on her work with renewed intensity. She was determined to move forward; to rebuild the walls she had so carefully constructed before Lawrence had come into her life. The promotion she received, a direct result of her contributions to the project, was a recognition of her talent and hard work. But like Lawrence, she found that the victory felt hollow. The joy she should have felt was overshadowed by the emptiness left their decision.

In the weeks that followed, they avoided each other as much as possible. Meetings were brief and to the point, emails were kept strictly professional, and any interaction outside of work was non-existent. The distance between them was necessary, but it was also painful. Every time they passed each other in the hallway, every time their hands brushed accidentally, they were reminded of what they had lost. Their lives outside of work were equally strained. Lawrence's family, still in Bangalore, noticed the change in his tone during their weekly phone calls. He was more withdrawn and less enthusiastic, even as he spoke of his professional successes.

His mother, ever perceptive, sensed that something was wrong, but Lawrence brushed off her concerns, insisting that he was simply busy with work. Advika, on the other hand, found herself more entangled in her family's expectations. Her parents pleased with her professional accomplishments, doubled down on their efforts to find her a suitable match. Advika went along with their plans, attending family gatherings and meeting potential suitors with polite interest, but her heart wasn't in it. The idea of beginning a new relationship, of letting someone into her world, felt daunting-almost unimaginable.

As time passed, Lawrence and Advika began to process the events of the past few months. The pain of their separation didn't disappear, but it began to transform into something different – a catalyst for personal growth. The experience forced Lawrence to confront some uncomfortable truths about himself. His ambition, which had always driven him forward, had also blinded him to what was truly important. In his quest for professional success, he had pushed aside his emotional needs, convincing himself that career advancement would bring him happiness. But now, with his career on an upward trajectory and his personal life in shambles, he realised how misguided that belief had been.

Lawrence began to reflect on his choices, questioning whether his sacrifices were worth it. He started to explore his interests outside of work, reconnecting with old hobbies and trying to meet new people. It wasn't easy – Delhi was still a city that felt foreign to him, and the loneliness he had felt when he first arrived had only intensified. But Lawrence was determined to find a sense of balance, to rediscover the parts of himself that he had neglected in his pursuit of success.

Advika's journey of personal growth was similarly challenging. The decision to end her relationship with Lawrence had forced her to confront the societal and familial expectations that had always dictated her life. She had spent so much of her life trying to be the perfect daughter, the perfect employee, the perfect woman that she had lost sight of who she really was. Advika began to question the path that had been laid out for her – the path that she had followed so dutifully for so many years. She started to push back against her family's expectations, asserting her independence in small but significant ways.

She declined their suggestions for arranged meetings, explaining that she wanted to focus on her career for now. She took up new hobbies, activities that had nothing to do with work or family but were purely for her own enjoyment. Slowly, Advika began to redefine her identity, separating herself from the roles that others had imposed on her. She started considering what she truly wanted out of life, independent of the pressures she had always felt. It was a difficult process that required her to confront her fears and insecurities head-on. But it was also liberating, allowing her to step into her own power and take control of her destiny.

Months passed, and the intensity of their emotions began to fade, replaced by a quiet acceptance of the choices they had made. Life moved on, as it always does, and both Lawrence and Advika found themselves slowly adjusting to their new realities. Then, one day, they crossed paths again – this time at a tech conference in Mumbai. It was a large event, filled with industry professionals from across the country, and neither had expected to see the other there. But as fate would have it, they found themselves in the same breakout session, sitting just a few rows apart.

At first, neither of them noticed the other, too focused on the presentation at hand. But when the session ended and the crowd began to disperse, Lawrence spotted Advika across the room. His heart skipped a beat, a familiar sensation he hadn't felt in months. He hesitated momentarily, unsure whether to approach her, but something inside him urged him forward. Advika, engrossed in conversation with a colleague, didn't see Lawrence until he was standing right in front of her. When she looked up and saw him, her breath caught in her throat, it had been so long since they had last seen each other, yet the connection between them was as strong as ever.

"Lawrence," she said, her voice a mix of surprise and warmth.

"Advika," he replied, smiling gently. "I didn't expect to see you here."

"Neither did I," she admitted, her eyes searching his face for signs of how he had been. "How have you been?"

"I've been…okay," Lawrence said, choosing his words carefully. "It's been a challenging few months, but I'm managing. And you?"

"Same," Advika replied, nodding slowly. "It's been a time of reflection, I suppose."

They stood there for a moment, the noise of the conference fading into the background as they focused on each other. The tension that had once existed between them was gone, replaced by something softer – an understanding, a shared history that had shaped them both in ways they were only beginning to comprehend.

"I'm glad to see you," Lawrence said finally, his voice sincere. "I've thought about you a lot."

"Me too," Advika admitted. "I've wondered how you were doing, but I didn't think it was my place to reach out."

Lawrence nodded, understanding the sentiment. "It's probably better that we didn't. But I'm glad we're here now."

"Yeah," Advika agreed, her smile tinged with a hint of sadness. "It's good to see you, Lawrence."

They talked for a few more minutes, catching up on the basics of their lives – work, family, the small details that fill the gaps in time. But neither of them mentioned the past, the choices they had made, or the feelings they had once shared. It was as if those memories were too fragile to touch, too significant to revisit. As the conference continued around them, they both knew that their encounter was fleeting. They were on different paths now, paths that had diverged when they made the decision to part ways. But there was no bitterness, no regret – only a quiet acceptance of what had been and what could have been. When they finally said their goodbyes, there was a sense of closure, a feeling that the chapter of their lives that had involved each other was truly behind them.

They walked away in different directions, their hearts lighter for having seen each other, for knowing that they had both found their way forward. As Lawrence and Advika returned to their respective lives, they carried with them the lessons they had learned from their time together. The experiences they had shared, the challenges they had faced, and the decisions they had made had shaped them into the people they were now. For Lawrence, the encounter with Advika served as a reminder of the importance of balance in life. He continued to pursue his career with the same dedication, but he also made time for the things that truly mattered to him – his family, his friends, and his own personal growth. He had come to realise that success was not just about climbing the corporate ladder, but about finding fulfilment in all aspects of life.

Advika, too, found herself more at peace after seeing Lawrence again. The encounter had reaffirmed her belief that she was on the right path – a path that was defined by her own choices, not by the expectations of others. She continued to excel in her career, but she also made time for the things that brought her joy and fulfilment. She had learned that she didn't have to sacrifice her own happiness for the sake of others and that she could define her own success on her own terms. As they both moved forward, the future remained uncertain. Their lives had taken different directions, and there was no telling where those paths would lead them. But the connection they had shared, however brief, had left a lasting impact on both of them – a reminder of the complexity of life, of love, and of the choices we make.

In the end, Lawrence and Advika's story was one of growth, of learning to navigate the challenges that life throws our way, and of finding the strength to move forward even when the road is difficult. Their relationship had been a test of their values, their priorities, and their ability to stay true to themselves. And while they had ultimately chosen to part ways, the lessons they had learned from each other would stay with them for the rest of their lives. Whether their paths would cross again in the future was a question left unanswered, a possibility that lingered in the air. But for now, they were content to continue on their separate journeys, knowing that they had both emerged stronger, wiser, and more certain of who they were and what they wanted out of life.

VI

As Lawrence and Advika each settled into the next chapter of their lives, they often found themselves reflecting on the choices they had made and the impact those choices had on their present and future. Lawrence, now more attuned to the importance of balance, sought out opportunities to mentor younger colleagues, sharing his experiences and helping them navigate the complexities of corporate life. He had learned that success wasn't just about achieving goals but also about maintaining integrity and staying true to one's values.

Advika, having redefined her sense of self, became a role model for other women in her industry, encouraging them to pursue their careers without compromising their personal happiness. She continued to push boundaries, both in her professional work and personal life, never losing sight of the lessons she had learned about independence and self-worth.

They both knew that the decisions they had made, though painful, were necessary for their growth. The love they had shared, brief as it was, had been a catalyst for change, pushing them to confront their fears and insecurities and ultimately leading them to a deeper understanding of themselves.

~ X ~ X ~ X ~ X ~ X ~ X ~ X ~ X ~ X ~ X ~ X ~ X ~ X ~ X ~ X ~

The story of Lawrence and Advika doesn't end with a definitive resolution, but rather with an open-ended question – a recognition that life is complex and that the choices we make often lead us down unexpected paths. As they each continued their journeys, the possibility of their paths crossing again remained, but it was not something either of them fixated on. They had found peace in the knowledge that they had done what was best for themselves, even if it meant letting go of something that had once meant so much to them.

Their story is a reminder that life is full of uncertainties, but it is also full of possibilities. The future is unwritten, and the choices we make today shape the paths we will walk tomorrow. For Lawrence and Advika, the future was wide open – a landscape of potential waiting to be explored. And so, their story ends not with a conclusion but with a beginning – a beginning that is as uncertain as it is full of promise.

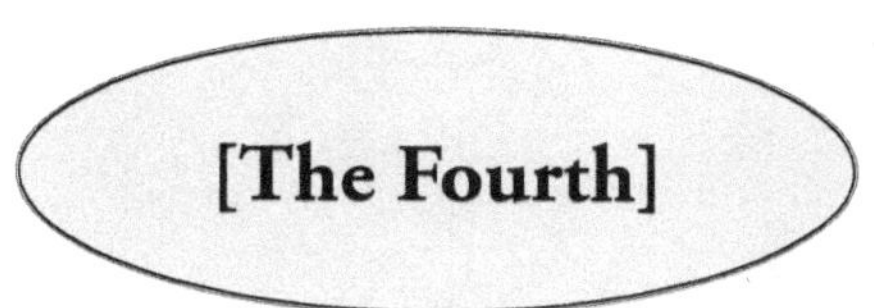

[The Fourth]

A Secret Between Us

Chapter 1

The Unexpected Rehearsal

Briar Costa leaned back in his chair, staring out the window of the high school principal's office. The muffled sound of students bustling in the hallways barely registered with him as he tried to ignore the stern gaze of Ms. Maggie, his English teacher, who was standing beside the principal, Father Alex. He knew this wasn't good – he'd crossed the line again. How many times had he been sent here? Four? Five?

"You need to take responsibility for your actions, Briar," Ms. Maggie said, her voice hard but not without a hint of frustration. "You've been disrupting class for weeks now. I'm tired of you wasting your potential." Briar rolled his eyes, barely concealing his boredom. "I'm not disrupting anything. I'm just bored." Father Alex cleared his throat. "Well, you've left us no choice but to find another way to 'engage' you." Briar's eyes flicked to the principal, finally curious. "What do you mean by 'another way'?" Ms. Maggie crossed her arms. "You're going to participate in the school's upcoming drama production." Briar blinked. Of all the things he'd expected, that wasn't it. "Drama? You want me to stand on a stage and pretend to care about some lame play?"

Father Alex leaned forward. "Yes, exactly. You've got too much energy, and you need an outlet. Drama will give you that. And if you refuse –" "Detention for the rest of the semester," Ms. Maggie finished with a smirk. Briar opened his mouth to argue but thought better of it. Detention meant sitting in a silent room doing nothing – pure torture. At least with drama, he'd be moving around, even if it meant doing something he'd never considered. "Fine," he said after a long pause. "I'll do it. But don't expect me to enjoy it." Ms. Maggie's smirk widened. "We don't expect anything. Just show up."

Later that afternoon, Briar reluctantly made his way to the school hall. He shoved his hands in his pockets and took in the scene before him. The stage was a chaotic flurry of activity – students arranging props, adjusting lights, and rehearsing lines. The drama teacher, Ms. Esther, was barking instructions as she tried to organise the madness. Briar sighed. This was going to be a long couple of months. "Hey, new guy!" Ms. Esther called from the stage. "Get over here!" Briar trudged forward, ignoring the curious stares of the other students. He wasn't exactly an unknown figure at school. People knew him for his reputation – popular, reckless, always on the verge of getting in trouble but never quite caring about the consequences. He didn't expect any of them to be happy he was joining the production.

As he approached, Ms. Esther introduced him to a small group of students who seemed to be key players in the production. "This is Briar Costa. He'll be joining the cast," Ms. Esther said, her tone making it clear that Briar's participation wasn't exactly voluntary. A few of the students exchanged glances, but one person caught Briar's attention – a girl standing a little apart from the others, her dark brown hair tied neatly in a ponytail. She was flipping through a script, barely acknowledging his presence. Her calm demeanour stood in stark contrast to the bustling energy around her. "And this," Ms. Esther continued, gesturing to the girl, "is Rinku Verde. She's playing the lead in the production."

At the mention of her name, Rinku looked up. Her eyes met Briar's briefly, a polite but distant smile forming on her lips. Then, without a word, she returned to her script. Briar raised an eyebrow. He wasn't used to being brushed off so easily. Most people, especially girls, gave him more attention than that. "Well, don't just stand there," Ms. Esther said, shoving a script into Briar's hands. "Get familiar with your lines. You'll be Rinku's partner in most of the scenes." "Lucky me," Briar muttered under his breath.

The first rehearsal was awkward, to say the least. Briar fumbled through his lines, completely out of his element, while Rinku delivered her performance with an effortless grace. It didn't take long for him to notice that Rinku was something of a perfectionist – she rarely made a mistake, and when she did, she corrected herself immediately without any fuss. Briar, on the other hand, struggled to take anything seriously. "Can we take this from the top?" Rinku asked after Briar flubbed a line for the third time in a row. Her tone was calm, but there was a hint of impatience beneath the surface.

Briar sighed, his frustration mounting. "Why? Does it really matter if I miss one word?"

"It does if you care about the play," Rinku replied coolly, her eyes narrowing slightly. "Well, I don't," Briar shot back. "I'm only here because I have to be." Rinku studied him momentarily before shaking her head, her expression unreadable. "Then maybe you should try to make the most of it." Something about her words – and the way she said them – rubbed Briar the wrong way. Who was she to tell him how to feel about this stupid play? But before he could snap back, Ms. Esther clapped her hands, signalling the end of the rehearsal. "That's it for today, everyone! We'll pick up where we left off tomorrow." Briar stuffed the script into his bag and started to head for the door, eager to put the day behind him, but a voice called out behind him.

"Briar." He turned to see Rinku standing a few feet away, her arms crossed over her chest. "What?" he asked, trying to keep his irritation in check. "I know you don't care about this right now," Rinku said, her voice soft but firm. "But you should at least try. For the sake of everyone else involved." Briar frowned, taken aback by her directness. Most people didn't bother calling him out like this. "Why do you care so much?" he asked, genuinely curious. Rinku hesitated for a moment before answering. "Because this play is important to me. I've worked hard on it, and I want to be good. So, if you're going to be part of it, I just ask that you put in some effort. That's all." With that, she turned and walked away, leaving Briar standing there with a mix of confusion and annoyance. He didn't get people like Rinku. Why was she so serious about everything? But as he watched her go, he couldn't shake the feeling that there was more to her than she let on.

Maybe this drama thing wouldn't be as straightforward as he thought.

CHAPTER 2

BEHIND THE CURTAIN

The school hall buzzed with activity the following afternoon, the hum of voices mixing with the clang of props and the shuffling of scripts. Briar leaned against the back wall, his arms crossed, eyes scanning the room. He still couldn't shake the strange conversation he'd had with Rinku the day before. Why did she care so much about this play? And why did it bother him that she did? Rehearsals weren't supposed to mean anything to him, but Rinku's quiet intensity had gotten under his skin. There was something about the way she carried herself, the way she focused on every detail as if it were the most important thing in the world. She was different from the other girls at school – serious, driven, and a little distant.

She hadn't even looked at him when she arrived today, too focused on flipping through her script. It shouldn't have bothered him, but it did. Briar wasn't used to being ignored. "Alright, everyone!" Ms. Esther's voice cut through the chatter, calling the rehearsal to order. "We're picking up where we left off yesterday. Briar, Rinku – get to the stage. You two are up first." Briar sighed, straightened up, and made his way toward the stage. Rinku was already there, waiting. As he stepped under the bright lights, he glanced over at her. She was standing perfectly still, script in hand, her eyes downcast as she mouthed the words to herself, as if she hadn't already memorised every line. "Let's take it from Scene Four, where Briar's character, James, confesses his feelings for Elena," Ms. Esther instructed. "Remember, Briar, this is a pivotal moment for your character. You've been holding back; now you finally let Elena see the real you."

Briar nodded, though he barely cared about his character's emotional arc. He glanced at Rinku again, trying to gauge her mood, but she was completely focused on the task at hand, as always. Her calm demeanour only made him feel more out of place. They began the scene with Rinku delivering her lines flawlessly; her voice filled with the appropriate mix of confusion and longing. Briar fumbled through his lines at first, but as the scene progressed, he found himself unexpectedly absorbed. It wasn't because of the script but because of Rinku. There was something magnetic about the way she acted – so controlled, yet so vulnerable at the same time. It was as if she became a different person on stage, and Briar couldn't look away.

For a moment, he forgot about the play and the forced nature of his involvement. He forgot about his usual nonchalance. In that brief instant, he wasn't Briar Costa, the rebellious popular kid. He was James, the guy hopelessly in love with Elena, torn between confessing his feelings or walking away. "I can't hide this anymore," Briar said, his voice unexpectedly soft and sincere. "Every time I see you, I want to tell you the truth. I'm tired of pretending. I – I love you, Elena." The words felt more real than he intended, and when he looked at Rinku, something flickered in her eyes. Was it surprise? Maybe even admiration? For a brief second, Briar thought he saw her break character, her perfectly crafted façade cracking ever so slightly. But just as quickly, it was gone.

"That was… better," Rinku said, barely glancing his way as the scene ended. She gathered her things and moved to the side of the stage without another word, as if nothing out of the ordinary had happened. Briar frowned. Better? That's all she had to say? He was starting to realise that getting any kind of real reaction out of her was going to be a lot harder than he thought.

Later that evening, Briar lingered after rehearsal, watching as the other students packed up and left. Most of them were laughing and chatting, clearly enjoying themselves. But not Rinku. She was sitting alone on the edge of the stage, flipping through her script once again, as if there was still something to perfect. Her determination was admirable, but it also seemed a little lonely. For reasons he couldn't quite explain, Briar found himself walking toward her. "You're really dedicated to this, aren't you?" he asked, hopping up onto the stage beside her. Rinku glanced at him briefly before returning her attention to the script. "I want it to be good." Briar waited for her to say more, but she didn't. She just kept flipping through the pages, her face unreadable.

"You know," he said, trying again, "I've been wondering something." Rinku didn't look up, but he could tell she was listening. "You're always so focused on everything. The play, school, life. Don't you ever just…. relax?" This time, Rinku stopped reading. She lowered her script and looked at him, her expression guarded. "I have a lot of responsibilities," she said after a long pause. "To the play?" Briar asked, raising an eyebrow. Rinku shook her head. "To my family." Briar didn't press her, sensing that she wasn't going to elaborate.

But her answer only deepened the mystery around her. What kind of responsibilities could she be talking about? What was weighing her down so much that she couldn't even relax during rehearsals? Before he could ask anything else, Rinku stood up, gathering her things. "I should go. See you tomorrow." Briar watched her leave, a growing curiosity gnawing at him. Rinku wasn't like anyone he'd ever met before, and he couldn't shake the feeling that there was more to her than she was letting on.

The next few days of rehearsal followed a similar pattern. Briar did his best to keep up with the script, but he was constantly distracted by Rinku. She never seemed to let her guard down. Even when they shared a laugh with the rest of the cast or worked through a difficult scene, she always kept a certain distance. One afternoon, after rehearsal had ended, Briar spotted Rinku slipping away from the school hall, her shoulders tense. Something about her posture told him that she wasn't just in a hurry – she was upset. Without thinking, Briar followed her, weaving through the nearly empty hallways until he saw her duck into an empty classroom. He hesitated outside the door, unsure if he should intrude. But then he heard a soft sound – a muffled sob. His heart twisted in a way he didn't expect. Before he could talk himself out of it, he knocked gently on the door.

"Rinku?" There was a pause, then the sound of hurried footsteps. A moment later, Rinku opened the door, her face pale, her eyes red. Briar was caught off guard. He had never seen her like this – so vulnerable. It was a stark contrast to the composed, almost aloof girl he'd been rehearsing with for weeks. "I'm fine," she said quickly, trying to push past him. But Briar stepped in her way, his concern outweighing his usual indifference. "Are you?" Rinku blinked, clearly taken aback by his persistence. For a moment, she looked like she was going to shut him out again, but then her shoulders slumped. "I don't... I don't want to talk about it," she said, her voice barely above a whisper. Briar didn't push. Instead, he sat down on one of the desks and nodded toward the chair beside him. "You don't have to talk. But if you want to sit for a bit…. I'll stay."

Rinku hesitated, clearly torn between her instinct to keep everything bottled up and the weight of whatever she was carrying. Finally, she sat down, wiping her eyes with the back of her hand. For a long time, they sat in silence, the tension between them slowly easing. Briar didn't say a word, and neither did she. But something about the quietness of the moment felt important, like they'd crossed a threshold neither of them had expected. Eventually, Rinku broke the silence, her voice shaky but determined. "I have a lot of things going on right now," she said, staring down at her hands. "Things I can't talk about. Not with anyone." Briar didn't push her to explain. He didn't need to. For the first time, he saw Rinku for who she really was – not the perfect student, not the minister's daughter, but someone who was struggling just like everyone else. Someone who had her own fears, her own secrets.

And in that moment, he realised just how much he wanted to know her. Not just the version of her she showed to the world, but the real Rinku Verde, the one behind the curtain.

-135-

CHAPTER 3

THE HIDDEN HEART

Briar couldn't stop thinking about Rinku. Ever since that quiet, tense moment in the empty classroom, something had shifted between them, at least for him. He had seen a side of her that no one else seemed to notice – the cracks in her perfectly composed exterior. And the more he thought about it, the more he realised that Rinku wasn't just some uptight, focused girl who took everything too seriously. There was something deeper, something she was keeping hidden, and it gnawed at him. He still didn't know what it was. Whatever secret Rinku was guarding, she wasn't ready to share it yet.

But after that day, Briar felt himself drawn to her in a way he hadn't anticipated. And the more time they spent together at rehearsals, the more he realised how much he enjoyed being around her. Not that Rinku made it easy. She still kept her distance, especially when they weren't rehearsing their scenes. But Briar noticed the little things – the way she would glance at him when she thought he wasn't looking, the way her voice softened when they spoke off-script, the brief moments when she let her guard slip, even if only for a second. It was driving him crazy. He wanted to break through that wall she had built, but he didn't know how.

The next week, rehearsals ramped up as the play's opening night approached. Ms. Esther pushed the cast hard, running scene after scene, adjusting lines, blocking, and refining performances. Briar found himself surprisingly invested, though he wasn't sure if it was the play itself or the chance to spend more time with Rinku that kept him showing up. Either way, it was working. One afternoon, after a particularly exhausting rehearsal, Briar and Rinku found themselves alone on the stage. The rest of the cast had filtered out, but Rinku lingered, as she often did, reviewing her lines and adjusting her movements in front of an imaginary audience. Briar watched her for a moment, his hands shoved in his pockets, before making his way over to her. "You ever take a break?" he asked, his voice light, though he meant the question.

Rinku glanced up, her expression calm, but there was a hint of amusement in her eyes. "I take breaks," she replied, though it sounded like she was trying to convince herself as much as him. "Uh-huh," Briar said, raising an eyebrow. "When's the last time you did something that wasn't on your to-do list?" Rinku frowned, looking slightly confused. "What do you mean?" "You know, fun," Briar said, waving his hands around as if it should be obvious. "Something spontaneous, something that isn't planned down to the last detail. Don't you ever just... do something because you feel like it?" Rinku's frown deepened, as if she were genuinely considering his question. "I have responsibilities, Briar," she said finally. "I can't afford to just do things because I feel like it."

"That's what you said last time," Briar pointed out. "But seriously, don't you ever want to just break out of the routine? Do something that's not expected?" Rinku hesitated, then shook her head. "I have a plan for my life, Briar. A list of things I need to accomplish, things I need to focus on. I don't have the luxury of being… careless." Briar leaned against the stage; his curiosity piqued. "What kind of list? What's on it?" Rinku's expression shifted, becoming more guarded. She looked down at her hands, fidgeting with the edges of her script. "It's just things I want to achieve," she said vaguely. "Things that are important to me." "Like what?" Briar pressed, sensing she was holding back.

Rinku hesitated again, then finally met his gaze. "Like going to college, getting a degree, helping my father with his work at the church. My family has expectations, Briar. I can't let them down." Briar was silent for a moment, trying to process what she was saying. He'd known about Rinku's father, of course – everyone in town did. Pastor Verde was a well-respected figure, a man of unwavering principles and high expectations for his daughter. But hearing Rinku talk about it like this, as if her entire life was mapped out for her, made Briar feel uneasy. "What about what you want?" he asked quietly. "Is that on the list?" Rinku's expression tightened, her eyes hardening just a bit. "What I want doesn't matter as much as what I have to do." Briar opened his mouth to argue, but Rinku stood up suddenly, cutting him off.

"Look, I appreciate the concern, but I'm fine," she said, her voice brisk. "This is just how things are for me. I can handle it." Briar watched her gather her things, feeling frustrated. He wanted to say more, to push her to open up, but he could see that she wasn't going to let him in. Not yet. "I get that you're busy," he said, trying to keep his tone light. "But maybe sometimes you should let yourself have a little fun. You know, go off-script for once." Rinku glanced at him, her expression softening slightly. "I'll think about it," she said quietly before walking away, leaving Briar standing alone on the stage.

A few days later, Briar found himself sitting outside the school hall after school, flipping through his script without really paying attention to the words. His mind kept drifting back to Rinku – her calm, composed exterior, the way she seemed to carry the weight of the world on her shoulders. He wanted to understand her better, but every time he got close, she pulled away. "Hey, Briar," a voice called out, breaking his thoughts. He looked up to see his friend Seph walking over, a knowing grin on his face. "You're really getting into this drama thing, huh?" Briar shrugged. "Yeah, it's not as bad as I thought. Beats detention, at least." Seph smirked, sitting down beside him. "Uh-huh. Sure. I'm sure it's got nothing to do with a certain someone in the cast." Briar shot him a look. "What are you talking about?"

"Come on, man," Seph said, elbowing him playfully. "You've been spending a lot of time with Rinku lately. You're not fooling anyone." Briar sighed, leaning back against the wall. "It's not like that." "Really?" Seph raised an eyebrow. "Because it looks like you've got a thing for her." Briar was silent for a moment, unsure how to respond. Did he have a thing for Rinku? He wasn't even sure himself. All he knew was that she was different, and that difference fascinated him. He couldn't stop thinking about her, couldn't stop wondering what went on behind those guarded eyes. "I don't know, man," Briar said finally. "It's complicated."

Seph nodded, his grin fading as he sensed the shift in Briar's mood. "She's got a lot going on, huh?" Briar ran a hand through his hair, feeling the weight of it all. "Yeah. More than she lets on." Seph clapped him on the shoulder. "Well, if anyone can crack that shell, it's you. Just… be careful, okay?" Briar nodded, appreciating the advice, but he knew it wasn't going to be easy. There was something about Rinku, something deep and guarded, and he wasn't sure if he'd ever really get close enough to figure it out.

Later that week, Briar found himself alone with Rinku again after rehearsal. The rest of the cast had left, and the school hall was quiet, the stage lights casting long shadows across the empty seats. Rinku was sitting at the edge of the stage, as usual, her script in her lap. Briar walked over and sat beside her, unsure of what to say. "You really don't take breaks, do you?" he asked, trying to keep his tone light. Rinku glanced at him, her expression unreadable. "I don't have time for breaks." Briar frowned. "You keep saying that, but it sounds like you're just making excuses." Rinku's eyes flickered with something – anger, maybe, or frustration. "You don't understand, Briar. My life isn't like yours. I don't get to just… do whatever I want."

Briar's frown deepened. "What does that mean? What aren't you telling me?" Rinku looked away, her hands tightening around the edges of her script. "I can't talk about it." "Why not?" Briar asked, his voice softening. "Rinku, whatever it is, you don't have to carry it alone." Rinku's jaw clenched, her eyes filling with an emotion Briar couldn't quite place. "You don't get it," she said quietly. "You don't know what it's like to live with the kind of expectations I do. To have to be perfect all the time." Briar's heart twisted at the pain in her voice. He didn't know what she was going through, not exactly, but he wanted to. He wanted to help.

"Then tell me," he said, his voice almost pleading. "Let me in." For a moment, it looked like Rinku might finally open up. Her eyes met his, and Briar saw the vulnerability there, the fear and uncertainty she kept hidden from everyone else. But then, just as quickly, the walls went back up. Rinku stood abruptly, gathering her things. "I have to go," she said, her voice distant again. Briar watched her walk away, frustration and confusion swirling inside him. Whatever secret Rinku was hiding was tearing her apart. And no matter how hard he tried, she wouldn't let him in. But Briar wasn't ready to give up. Not yet.

CHAPTER 4

CRACKS IN THE FAÇADE

The tension between Briar and Rinku was palpable. Every day, they worked together, rehearsing the same scenes over and over, but there was an invisible barrier between them now, something unspoken that hung in the air like a heavy fog. Briar was growing more frustrated by the day. No matter how much he tried to get closer to her, to understand what was really going on behind those guarded eyes, Rinku kept him at arm's length. It was exhausting. He had never wanted to know someone as much as he wanted to know Rinku Verde. And yet, she was the most distant person he'd ever met. Her smile was polite but never warm. Her words were friendly, but she never revealed anything truly personal. It was like she had built a fortress around herself, and every time Briar got close, she pulled the drawbridge up, locking him out.

One afternoon, after yet another rehearsal filled with awkward pauses and lingering silences, Briar couldn't take it anymore. They were practising a scene where James, his character, was supposed to pour his heart out to Elena, Rinku's character, but the emotion just wasn't there. Not because of the script but because of the wall Rinku kept between them. "That was... flat," Ms. Esther said from her seat in the audience, shaking her head. "Come on, you two, this is the emotional climax of the play! Briar, you're in love with her. Rinku, you're conflicted, but deep down, you feel the same way. I need to see that!" Briar gritted his teeth, glancing at Rinku, who stood with her script clutched in her hands, her face expressionless. They were supposed to be in love, but how was he supposed to convey that when she wouldn't even look him in the eye? "Let's run it again," Ms. Esther said with a sigh, clearly frustrated.

Briar took a deep breath, trying to focus on the lines, but his mind kept drifting to Rinku. Why wouldn't she just let him in? Why did she keep herself so distant, so separate from everyone else? The question gnawed at him, distracting him from the script. "You have no idea what this has cost me," Briar said, his character's voice breaking with emotion. "I can't keep pretending anymore, Elena. I love you, and I don't care who knows it." Rinku's response was slow, her voice flat, as if she were reading from a textbook instead of pouring her heart out. "But you don't understand. We can't... it's not that simple." Briar snapped, the frustration boiling over into his performance. "Why isn't it that simple? What's stopping you? Why are you so afraid to let me in?" His outburst wasn't part of the script, but it felt real, too real. It wasn't James asking Elena—it was Briar asking Rinku. And judging by the way her eyes widened slightly, she knew it, too.

There was a long, uncomfortable silence, and Ms. Esther finally stood up, clapping her hands. "Alright, that's enough for today. We'll work on this scene tomorrow. Briar and

Rinku, I need more from both of you. You're holding back, and it's showing. Go home and think about your characters." As the rest of the cast began to pack up, Briar stayed on stage, his chest heaving with barely controlled frustration. He glanced at Rinku, who was methodically folding her script, her face as calm and collected as ever. It was infuriating. How could she act so composed after what had just happened? Briar walked over to her, his hands clenching into fists at his sides. "What's your deal, Rinku?" he asked, his voice low but edged with anger. Rinku looked up at him, her expression unreadable. "What do you mean?" "You know exactly what I mean," Briar said, taking a step closer. "You're holding back. You're not giving me anything to work with, on stage or off. You're acting like none of this matters."

Rinku's eyes flashed with something - anger, maybe, or defensiveness - but she quickly masked it. "I'm doing my best." "No, you're not," Briar shot back, his frustration spilling over. "You're just going through the motions. You're treating this like it's just another task on your list, and it's driving me crazy." Rinku stiffened, her face hardening. "You don't know anything about what I'm dealing with, Briar." "Then tell me," Briar said, his voice rising. "Tell me what's really going on with you. I'm sick of the fake smiles and the polite responses. I want to know the real Rinku, not the one who's pretending everything's fine all the time." For a moment, Rinku said nothing. She stared at him, her eyes filled with something raw and vulnerable, but then she shook her head, her lips pressing into a thin line. "You don't understand."

"I'm trying to," Briar said, his voice softening. "But you won't let me." Rinku looked away, her hands trembling slightly as she gathered her things. "It's not that simple, Briar. I can't just tell you everything." "Why not?" Briar asked, stepping in front of her before she could leave. "What are you so afraid of?" Rinku's eyes flicked up to meet his, and for a brief moment, Briar thought she might finally tell him. But then, just as quickly, the moment passed. She pulled her bag over her shoulder and shook her head. "I have to go." And just like that, she was gone, leaving Briar standing alone on the stage, his frustration and confusion swirling inside him like a storm. Over the next few days, the tension between Briar and Rinku only grew. They continued rehearsing together, but there was a noticeable strain in their interactions. Briar tried to be patient and give her space, but it was becoming harder to ignore the growing distance between them.

One evening, after a particularly tense rehearsal, Briar found himself wandering the empty halls of the school, his mind racing. He couldn't stop thinking about Rinku, about the way she had shut him out again. He hated feeling this helpless, hated not knowing what was going on with her. As he turned a corner, he heard voices coming from one of the classrooms. He recognised the soft, measured tone of Rinku's voice immediately. Curiosity piqued, Briar crept closer, staying just out of sight. "I don't know if I can keep this up," Rinku was saying, her voice heavy with emotion. "I thought I could handle it, but it's getting harder every day." Briar's heart skipped a beat. Who was she talking to? He inched closer, peering around the corner. Inside the classroom, Rinku was sitting at a desk, her head in her hands. Across from her sat another girl - Leila, one of her close friends from the drama club.

"I don't understand why you don't just tell Briar," Leila said softly. "He's been trying to get close to you. He deserves to know the truth." Rinku shook her head, her voice barely above a whisper. "I can't. If he knew... if anyone knew, it would ruin everything." Briar's stomach tightened. What truth? What was Rinku hiding? Leila leaned forward; her expression filled with concern. "You can't keep this secret forever, Rinku. It's only going to hurt more the longer you wait." Rinku wiped at her eyes, her voice trembling. "I don't know what to do. My family... they have so many expectations. And if this gets out, it could destroy everything my father's worked for." Briar's heart sank as realisation hit him like a tidal wave. Whatever Rinku was hiding, it wasn't just about her. It was about her family, about her father's reputation. And she had been carrying the weight of it all alone.

He took a step back, his mind racing. He didn't want to eavesdrop any longer, but the pieces of the puzzle were starting to fall into place. Rinku wasn't distant because she didn't care—she was distant because she cared too much. She was protecting something, something big, and it was tearing her apart. The next day, Briar couldn't focus during rehearsal. His mind was filled with the conversation he had overheard, the weight of Rinku's secret pressing down on him. He wanted to confront her, to tell her he knew, but he also knew that wasn't the right approach. If Rinku was going to open up, it had to be on her terms. As the rehearsal ended, Briar lingered backstage, watching as Rinku gathered her things. She looked tired, more so than usual, and Briar's heart ached for her. She was carrying so much, and no one even knew. "Rinku," he said softly as she walked past him. She stopped, turning to face him. "What is it?"

Briar hesitated, searching for the right words. "I... I just wanted to say that I'm here if you need to talk. About anything." Rinku's expression softened, but there was still a guardedness in her eyes. "Thanks, Briar. But I'm fine." Briar sighed. "You keep saying that, but I don't believe you." Rinku looked away, her hands tightening around the strap of her bag. "I can handle it." "I know you can," Briar said gently. "But you don't have to handle it alone." For a moment, Rinku stood there, her eyes locked on his, and Briar thought she might finally open up. But then, just like every other time, she pulled back. "I have to go."

And once again, she walked away, leaving Briar standing alone, the weight of her secret hanging heavy in the air between them.

CHAPTER 5

THE TRUTH COMES OUT

The evening of the play's opening night arrived with a strange mix of excitement and tension. The auditorium was alive with the buzz of students rushing around, setting up the last-minute props and making sure their costumes were perfect. But Briar could barely focus on any of it. His mind was still stuck on Rinku and the secret she had been hiding from him, from everyone. He glanced over at her as she stood near the side of the stage, going over her lines one last time, looking poised and collected as always. She wore her costume—a simple, elegant gown that made her look even more graceful than usual. But no matter how calm she appeared on the outside; Briar knew there was a storm raging beneath the surface. He had seen it in the small moments, in the cracks that were starting to show.

Briar still hadn't confronted her about what he had overheard, though it had taken everything in him not to. He had wanted to give her the chance to tell him on her own terms, to let her trust him enough to open up. But now, standing here on the night of their big performance, Briar wasn't sure she ever would. Maybe he had been foolish to think that Rinku would ever let him in. He took a deep breath, trying to push the thoughts away. They had a play to get through first, and despite everything, Briar knew how important this night was for Rinku. She had poured her heart into this production, and he owed it to her to make sure it went off without a hitch. "Places, everyone!" Ms. Esther called out from behind the curtain. "We're starting in five minutes!"

Briar watched as the rest of the cast took their positions, his heart pounding in his chest. This was it. Months of rehearsals, hours of frustration, tension, and moments of connection—all of it was coming to a head tonight. And somehow, it felt like more than just a play was at stake. The first act flew by in a blur. Briar and Rinku performed their scenes with precision, moving through their lines and stage directions like clockwork. On the outside, everything seemed perfect. The audience was engaged, laughing at the light-hearted moments, growing silent during the more dramatic ones. But for Briar, something felt off. He could feel the distance between him and Rinku, the weight of her secret hanging between them like a wall. Every time he looked into her eyes, he saw the mask she wore, the one that kept her real emotions hidden. And it was driving him crazy.

By the time they reached the final act, Briar was barely holding it together. The last scene was the emotional climax of the play - the moment when James confessed his love for Elena, the moment when everything was supposed to fall into place. But as Briar stood on the stage, staring at Rinku, he couldn't get the words out. "I... I can't keep pretending anymore," Briar said, his voice shaky, his heart pounding. "I love you, Elena. I've always loved you." Rinku responded perfectly; her voice soft but filled with emotion. "James, I... I don't know what to say. This is all so sudden." But Briar couldn't focus on the lines anymore. He wasn't just James standing on that stage. He was Briar, standing in front of Rinku, desperately wanting her to understand. He wanted to break through the façade, to get to the real person underneath. "I know you're scared," Briar said, his voice breaking slightly. "But you don't have to be. You don't have to carry this alone."

The words weren't in the script, but they came out anyway, raw and unfiltered. Rinku's eyes widened for a brief second, her composure faltering, and Briar could see the flicker of panic behind her eyes. She knew what he was doing. "I can't...," Rinku began, her voice shaking for the first time all night. "You don't understand..." "Then make me understand," Briar interrupted, taking a step closer to her. "Tell me the truth. Stop hiding behind this. I want to know the real you, Rinku." The audience was silent, completely unaware that they were witnessing something that had nothing to do with the play. Briar didn't care. He couldn't hold back anymore. Rinku stared at him, her breathing uneven, her eyes searching his for a way out. But there wasn't one. Not this time. "I can't," she whispered, her voice barely audible. "If you knew the truth, you'd never look at me the same way."

Briar's heart twisted at the vulnerability in her voice, but he didn't back down. "Try me." For a long moment, there was nothing but silence between them. The tension was unbearable, and Briar could see the struggle playing out in Rinku's eyes. She wanted to tell him. He knew she did.

But something was holding her back—something bigger than either of them. Finally, Rinku took a deep breath, her shoulders trembling as she spoke. "It's my family," she said, her voice trembling. "They... they've spent years building this perfect image, this reputation in the town. My father... he's a respected minister. Everyone looks up to him. But there's something they don't know." Briar's heart pounded in his chest as he listened, every word pulling him deeper into the truth he had been searching for.

"Last year," Rinku continued, her voice growing quieter with every word, "I was involved in something... something that could ruin everything. My father's reputation and our family's standing in the community would all fall apart if people found out. They've been keeping it quiet, hiding it, but I can't forget. I can't escape it." Briar felt like the ground had shifted beneath him. He had known Rinku was hiding something, but he hadn't expected this secret to be so heavy that it could tear her family apart. "What happened?" Briar asked gently, his voice barely above a whisper. Rinku swallowed hard, her eyes filling with unshed tears. "I made a mistake," she whispered. "I got involved with someone I shouldn't have. It was a scandal, something that could have destroyed my father's career. My family covered it up, but I've been living with the guilt ever since."

Briar's chest tightened as he saw the pain written all over her face. She had been carrying this alone for so long, pretending everything was fine while the weight of her secret slowly crushed her. "Rinku," Briar said softly, reaching out to her. "You're not your mistakes. And you're not your family's reputation. That doesn't define who you are." Rinku shook her head, a tear slipping down her cheek. "You don't understand. If this gets out, it won't just ruin me. It will ruin them." Briar's heart ached for her, but he couldn't stand to see her trapped like this anymore. He had fallen for her—not the perfect, composed girl she pretended to be, but the real Rinku, the one who was scared and vulnerable and carrying too much. He wasn't going to let her keep suffering in silence.

"I don't care about what happened," Briar said firmly. "I care about you. And I'm not going to walk away just because you made a mistake. You don't have to be perfect, Rinku. Not with me." For the first time, Briar saw something break in Rinku's eyes. The mask she had been wearing for so long crumbled, and she finally let the tears fall. Briar stepped forward, pulling her into his arms, holding her as she cried. The audience was still completely silent, unsure if what they were witnessing was part of the play or something real. But at that moment, Briar didn't care. All that mattered was Rinku and the fact that she had finally let him in.

After the curtain fell and the applause echoed throughout the auditorium, Briar and Rinku stood backstage, the weight of the performance and the confession still hanging between them. The rest of the cast was celebrating, but Briar barely noticed. His mind was still reeling from everything Rinku had told him, from the raw emotion of their last scene together. Rinku stood a few feet away, her arms wrapped around herself as if she were trying to hold herself together. Briar walked over to her; his heart still heavy with everything she had revealed. "You didn't have to tell me everything," Briar said softly, his voice filled with understanding. "But I'm glad you did." Rinku looked up at him, her eyes still red from crying. "I didn't mean to do it on stage," she said quietly. "It just... it all came out." Briar nodded, stepping closer. "Sometimes that's what happens when you keep something bottled up for so long. It has to come out eventually."

Rinku's eyes searched his as if she were still waiting for him to judge her and pull away. But Briar didn't. He had never felt more certain of anything in his life. "Briar," she whispered, her voice breaking, "I'm scared." "I know," Briar said softly, reaching out to take her hand. "But you're not alone anymore. I'm here." Rinku's lips trembled, and for the first time, she let herself lean into him, let herself be vulnerable. And in that moment, Briar knew that this was the real Rinku—the one who had been hidden behind the façade for so long. And he loved her even more for it.

CHAPTER 6

LOVE AND REDEMPTION

The days after the play were quieter than Briar expected. The whirlwind of emotions from that night still lingered in the air, but now, the aftermath felt like a strange calm settling over him. The play had been a success, with everyone talking about the raw and emotional performances, but Briar knew that what had happened on stage had nothing to do with acting. Rinku had bared her soul to him in front of everyone, and since then, she had kept her distance. She had been absent from school for a couple of days, and every time Briar asked one of their mutual friends if they had seen her, he got vague responses. It wasn't like Rinku to disappear, but after what had happened, he understood why.

Still, Briar couldn't shake the feeling that Rinku was pulling away. And this time, it wasn't because she was hiding her secret. She had finally told him the truth, but now it felt like she was retreating, afraid of what that truth meant for their relationship. One afternoon, after school, Briar found himself walking to Rinku's house. He wasn't sure what he was going to say or even if she would want to see him, but he knew he couldn't leave things unresolved. He had seen the real Rinku, the one behind the perfect façade, and he wasn't ready to let her disappear from his life without a fight.

As he approached her house, the familiar feeling of nervousness settled in his stomach. The large, stately home stood at the edge of town, surrounded by a perfectly manicured lawn. It was exactly the kind of place you would expect the town's minister to live, a house that radiated respectability and order. But now, knowing what Rinku had been carrying all this time, it felt suffocating. Briar walked up the steps and knocked on the door, his heart pounding in his chest. For a moment, there was nothing but silence, and he almost turned to leave. But then the door opened, and Rinku stood there, her eyes wide with surprise. "Briar," she said softly, her voice filled with a mixture of emotions. "What are you doing here?" "I needed to see you," Briar said, his voice steady despite the nerves swirling inside him. "We didn't get to talk after the play. And I don't want to leave things like this."

Rinku hesitated, glancing over her shoulder as if she was checking to see if anyone else was home. Then she stepped aside, opening the door wider to let him in. "Come inside." Briar followed her into the house, the air inside cool and quiet. The living room was just as formal and neat as he remembered, decorated with carefully chosen furniture and religious memorabilia. Everything was in its proper place, just like the image Rinku's family had worked so hard to maintain. They sat on the couch, and for a moment, neither spoke. The silence between them felt heavy, filled with all the things they hadn't said since that night. "I didn't expect to see you," Rinku said finally, her voice soft and unsure. Briar turned to face her, his expression gentle. "Why have you been avoiding me?" Rinku lowered her eyes, her hands fidgeting in her lap. "I wasn't sure if you'd want to see me after... everything."

Briar's heart ached at her words. She still didn't get it. She still didn't understand that her secret, her past didn't change how he felt about her. "Rinku," he said, reaching out to take her hand. "You're still the same person I've been falling for. What happened before... it doesn't change that." Rinku's eyes filled with tears, but she shook her head, pulling her hand away. "You say that now, but you don't understand what it's like. My whole life has been about living up to my family's expectations, to this perfect image they've built. And now... I've ruined that." Briar leaned forward, his voice firm but kind. "You haven't ruined anything. You made a mistake, Rinku, and you've paid for it by carrying that guilt around for so long. But it doesn't define who you are." Rinku's lip trembled, and she wiped at her eyes, trying to hold back the tears. "I don't know how to let go of it. I've spent so long hiding it, trying to be perfect, that I don't even know who I am anymore."

Briar's heart broke at her words. He could see the pain and confusion in her eyes, the weight of years of pressure and expectation finally taking its toll. But he also saw something else, something stronger. Rinku wasn't just the person her family wanted her to be. She was more than that, and; he wanted her to see it too. "You don't have to be perfect," Briar said softly, his voice filled with emotion.

"Not for me, not for anyone. You're enough just the way you are. The real you, the one I've been getting to know, the one who's scared and strong at the same time, that's who I care about. Not the perfect image you've been trying to live up to." Rinku looked up at him, her eyes shining with unshed tears. For a moment, there was nothing but silence between them, the air heavy with the weight of everything that had been left unsaid. And then, slowly, she nodded.

"I don't know if I can just let it all go," Rinku whispered, her voice shaky but determined. "But I want to try. I don't want to keep pretending." Briar smiled, his chest filling with relief and warmth. "That's all I'm asking. We'll figure it out together, one step at a time." For the first time in what felt like forever, Rinku smiled, a real, genuine smile. It was small, but it was enough to show Briar that she was finally starting to let her guard down.

Over the next few weeks, things between Briar and Rinku changed in ways Briar hadn't anticipated. They started spending more time together outside of school, not just rehearsing but getting to know each other. Rinku opened up little by little, sharing parts of herself that she had kept hidden for so long. Briar listened, never pushing, always letting her set the pace. It wasn't easy. Rinku still struggled with the weight of her past, the guilt and the fear of what would happen if her secret got out. But for the first time, she wasn't carrying it alone. Briar was there, standing by her side, helping her see that she didn't have to be perfect, that she was worthy of love and acceptance just as she was.

And somewhere along the way, they found something neither of them had expected happiness. It wasn't the fairy-tale kind of happiness that came with perfect endings or grand gestures. It was quieter, more subtle, built on trust and understanding. It was the kind of happiness that came from knowing that they could face whatever came next together, without hiding or pretending. One afternoon, as they sat on the steps of the school after the final drama club meeting, Rinku pulled out a small piece of paper from her bag. Briar glanced at it curiously. "What's that?" he asked, leaning in to get a better look. Rinku smiled softly, unfolding the paper to reveal a list written in neat, precise handwriting. "It's my to-do list," she said, her voice tinged with a hint of nostalgia. "I made it years ago, everything I thought I needed to do to live up to my family's expectations."

Briar looked at the list, reading the items she had written: **Get into a top college. Be the perfect daughter. Help with my father's church. Make no mistakes.** Rinku sighed, her smile fading. "I've been following this list for so long, trying to be perfect. But now... I think it's time to let it go." With a determined look in her eyes, Rinku tore the paper in half, the sound of it ripping through the air like a weight being lifted from her shoulders. Briar watched, feeling a sense of pride and admiration for her. "You don't need that list anymore," Briar said softly. "You've got your own path to follow." Rinku smiled again, this time wider and more genuine than before. "Yeah. I think I do." And as they sat there, side by side, watching the sun set over the town, Briar knew that whatever came next—whatever challenges they faced, whatever secrets still lingered—they would face it together. Because for the first time in their lives, they weren't pretending anymore.

They were free to be themselves, and that was more than enough.

—THE END—

ABOUT THE AUTHOR

Brian Miranda, a seasoned specialist in archives and document management, has spent over 25 years mastering the intricacies of Document Lifecycle, KYC Management, Relocation Services, and Travel Management. With a robust professional background, Brian has managed documents for numerous prestigious clients, bringing a wealth of experience and attention to detail to his writing.

Currently serving as the Vice President of Operations for a semiconductor research and development company, Brian combines his professional acumen with a creative flair. In his free time, he volunteers with World Harvest Church Dubai, showcasing his dedication to community service and support.

An avid football and cricket player, Brian has not only competed in major tournaments across Mumbai but also captained and coached the St. John the Evangelist Church

Parish Football team for three successful years. This spirit of teamwork and perseverance permeates his writing.

Brian's debut book of short stories reflects his passion for storytelling. Drawing inspiration from real-life experiences and his vivid imagination, he weaves compelling narratives that captivate and engage readers. His writing style blends fiction with authentic experiences, creating relatable and intriguing tales.

Brian invites you to connect with him and share in the journey of his storytelling adventure. Follow his work and updates to stay engaged with his literary pursuits.

* 9 7 9 8 8 9 6 9 9 2 8 5 1 *